LIL RONNIE –

Prt.3

(TURNED TABLES)

By: ABDU SAMAD IBN AMMAR REDDICK

ISBN: 9798867825409

We Help You Self-Publish Your Book
Crystell Publications
PO BOX 8044 / Edmond – OK 73083
www.crystellpublications.com
(405) 414-3991

Printed in the USA

Authors Notes

Coming from my own tale of poverty, there is nothing I cannot tell you in regard to street life.

Living at a high risk was completely normal to me. Guns drugs violence was as regular as a drink of water, sadly said but it took prison for me to realize certain things about my lifestyle was just not right. Given a 235-month sentence for a Human Trafficking Offense no one could have told me there was still purpose in my life. To me I was buried alive by a true offense of STREET LIFE. Guilty for doing things I was taught to do.

Being in an environment where losing yourself was easy I took on drowning myself with time so that I wouldn't be drowned in it.

My days consisted of building. Reading studying is growing because in truth the only thing placed me here was a lack of knowledge. I became one of the brothers on the yard who started professing change. Every day I was transferring myself into something more legitimate. My first step so happens to be my change of faith. I took away believing in myself and submitted to Allah. One book on the Deen of Islam gave me firm peace. In time my pride was replaced with knowledge and from there life became easy.

Entertaining the genre, I provide is actually frowned upon, Allah knows best, but writing is also a sense of peace for me. For the reader to know and understand that there was a time when the dope game was one of your few ways to escape poverty not so much the same today. There are tons of hustles better than the drug game and even promoting it like myself knows it.
Peace,

ABDU SAMAD IBN AMMAR REDDICK

ABDU SAMAD IBN AMMAR REDDICK

CHAPTER 1

Inside Blackman's BMW, Lil Ronnie sat quietly, listening to his attorney rush through problems he'd returned home to America to face. Kim, one of his baby mothers, had turned against him and surprisingly gave the law more than he could have ever anticipated. It was true, Lil Ronnie had killed her first child's father, but only with the necessary amount of cause. However, he also swept her under his wing, changing her and her son's lives for the better, so again, her cooperation was not something he could have predicted.

Through the windshield, Lil Ronnie watched the streetlights pass over them, bringing him closer to the federal building where he would soon be turning himself over to law enforcement. Managing to keep a clean record his entire life, Lil Ronnie did not know what to expect. What he did know is that Kim's decision had him between a dragon's mouth and a fly swapper, leaving him little to no room for escape. Nevertheless, Lil Ronnie remained confident, poised, and clear headed.

By the time Blackman finished speaking, Lil Ronnie's eyes were back on him. "So, paraphrasing what you're saying, basically, I'm fucked with her statement?"

"Yes," admitted Blackman as he continued driving. "Informants are the feds bread and butter. Without her testimony, they have nothing."

Nodding as his eyes shifted back out the window Lil Ronnie spoke as calmly as ever, "I can get rid of her. Make sure she's never found or some shit like that, right?"

Abruptly, Blackman turned his body in the driver's seat. "Are you insane!" he exclaimed. "You're already suspected of killing one informant; what you think killing another will do to you?"

"There's no other choice," Lil Ronnie pointed out.

"Kim is too valuable to them. She's already given too much," Blackman explained, his mind glued to Lil Ronnie's murderous comment. Blackman had learned long ago in his profession not to entertain his client's guilt. Hiring him meant they were innocent, which is what he put into his mind, but damn it, Lil Ronnie had made his guilt luminous. Taking a deep breath, Blackman cleared his own head, finding his famous lawyer smile. "Look, Ronnie, what you need is the exact opposite. Get her to change her statement somehow, but it has to be voluntarily. Her being alive and on your side guarantees freedom, can you make this happen?' Blackman asked.

The question lingered in the car all the way until arriving at the federal building, and at that time, Lil Ronnie had managed to sprout no reply. Relieving him of further thought, Blackman parked the BMW before stating, "Don't sweat it. As a conflict of interest, you'll be getting new counsel at your arraignment in the morning. Hazik wanted to be there and may still come but safety is best for everyone.

"What has Hazik said about all of this?" Lil Ronnie inquired while getting out of the car.

"He's pissed but receptive. Promised he'd turn every concert block over to get you out."

Nodding, Lil Ronnie walked with Blackman to the steel door and waited there for someone to come and get him.

$$$

Inside her office, Agent Pawlowski sorta hoped Lil Ronnie would go on a run instead of turning himself in. Leaning back in her seat, she thought of losing Selvester behind it all and wished he had never gotten her involved. She thought back to the day Selvester pranced into her office with all of his macho carousing antics like he still ran the place. Pawlowski hated him but not like she hated others. She hated him because she couldn't refuse him. Hated him because whatever he asked, she'd do even after he moved out and dumped her to marry Marcey. When he first presented the case to her, she had no interest. The case was just another building raid, however as things started to unravel it became interesting. First, Pawlowski became hard pressed on solving the murder of Lil Ronnie first baby mother. Then she came across something after digging into Selvester's wife's background and became even more enthralled. Realizing that another one of Lil Ronnie's baby mothers was Selvester's very own wife, a wife who happened to be the niece of the Rouhani family, pulled Pawlowski so far in that she practically became obsessed. The latest news, however, sent Selvester to an early death. A death Pawlowski took blame for after she had thrown Lil Ronnie and Marcey's relationship in his face. As she knew he would, Selvester raced home to confront Marcey but was later pronounced dead for a just cause. The news nearly shattered her, but doing what she does best, Pawlowski used her hurt to nail the case. She harassed, stocked, and created a massive research strategy that brought the case home, and as it was close to ending, she sadly realized it would be the end.

On her desk in the far-right corner, she answered the expected call. She told them she'd be right down, then placed another call to her partner, Brad. Meeting him as soon as she walked out of her office, the two walked step by step to the steel door where Lil Ronnie waited with his attorney.

Pawlowski opened the door for herself, intentionally letting her face be the first Lil Ronnie saw. When their eyes locked, Pawlowski smiled mirthfully. "Hello Ronnie, it's good to see you on my doorstep this time around," she teased before her thin lips turned into a tight line. "Cuff and send him through intake, Brad" Pawlowski ordered, breaking her eye contact.

Soon as the door was able to close, leaving her and Blackman alone, Pawlowski stepped closer, using a softer approach toward the attorney. "Any chance he breaks. The Rouhani family is not off our radar, and we'll be glad to trade.'

Blackman's tanned skin was twice as smooth, but the rings around his eyes exposed his age. In his mid-fifties, Pawlowski guessed as she waited for him to answer her question. His smirk was one of sophistication. Exuding power with a lot more finesse than Selvester. Having no problem using the tools it took, Pawlowski would have no problem sleeping with the attorney.

"Humph" she heard him groan before turning his back on her. "Go fuck yourself."

Pawlowski started to see the but quickly regained control, walking back inside the building smiling. Selvester's goal was accomplished. Lil Ronnie was upstairs getting booked-in, and only time stood between him going to trial, receiving a life sentence, and him changing the page to a new chapter.

$$$

The white wine was down to half a glass as Marcey sipped, using it to keep herself calm. It was something to see how the world could suddenly stop spinning. Receiving a call from one of her uncles after walking inside her home had done just that. Marcey sat there on her loveseat with her legs beneath her, wondering what news Hazik was bringing.

His distrust of phones pivoted the conversation into absolute wonder. Telling her nothing more than Lil Ronnie turning himself in. And it being a grave situation. Soon after, he hung up, telling her he was on his way. Marcey filled the glass and started drinking. The immediate impact shocked her because, as of late, her and Lil Ronnie's relationship had been almost nonexistent. She wouldn't allow him to see their child, and she even went to the extent of giving her body to someone else.

To her, Lil Ronnie cut off his safety valve the minute he refused her last warning to leave his other woman. She didn't expect to have a shock piercing her heart, or an urge to want him back out, but there she waited. When the doorbell sounded, Marcey took a deep breath and then walked over, letting her uncle in. Hazik, almost two inches shorter than her, looked up at her, releasing a warm smile. "Hello, my beautiful niece."

Returning the greeting, Marcey hugged him, then trailed behind as he made his way through the condo. His disposition showed a lot more poise than that of hers. There was no worry, no haste, just the usual normalcy that made her want to jump ahead and ask what the hell was going on. Controlling herself, Marcey thought of the discipline her family was built on and knew showing impatience would put a bad taste on her uncle's tongue. Keeping quiet as he walked around, she saw him look from the luxurious furnishings to her and Lil Ronnie's son's pictures. A sting floated through her body, knowing she had lied to her other uncles as well as Hazik about the relationship she had with Lil Ronnie, and although the cat was out of the bag, it was still fresh, and the lie would always exist.

"Eclipse, is his name correct?" She heard Hazik ask, stopping in front of one of his pictures. When she nodded, he said, 'Lil Ronnie promised to bring him by and introduce us."

"I should have told you I'm sorry, but-"

His hand waved at her, but Hazik did not turn from the photos. "I'm not mad, and dealing with your other uncles, I understand perfectly. Where is he?" he asked.

"We have a nanny who's usually here with him, but he's over with her tonight."

Sliding a hand inside his silk pants, she could hear her uncle jiggling the keys in his pocket. "I want to see him... soon," said Hazik, and Marcey knew her uncle was not asking. Shaking her head, she offered him a seat and then sat down after him.

"When were you notified of Lil Ronnie's arrest?" she asked.

Sighing deeply, Hazik said, 'I was aware before

he returned, didn't want to contact you until all the facts were lined up and he'd turned himself in."

"So Blackman knows something?"

"The agent bitch loves rubbing it in his face, something to do with Selvester, I'm guessing."

"Pawlowski?" Marcey asked. "What has she done? She doesn't know anything."

"Apparently, she know enough. Someone got the girl on a sale and manufacturing charge. Caused a raid on the house."

The arched brows of Marcey's crinkled. She knew all of Lil Ronnie's women like they knew her. Each one seemed to play a position that she hated because she could easily quench his every want. Depicting Tay and Kim's activities, Marcey knew it could only be Kim. "They tried to arrest her months ago. Raided the place but came up empty."

"I know, but there was a second raid days ago, Hazik said.

"Impossible Lil Ronnie cut her and that house out of the drug business until he got back. If it was open, it was something she did on her own."

Not one to dwell on the small things, Hazik moved on. The bottom line is that she's made herself a thorn. She's cooperating, and that will put Lil Ronnie away for God knows how long."

The hazel in Marcey's eyes twinkled with hate.

Meeting Lil Ronnie through Bell, she watched him practically grow as a child; however, even when he was, she never considered him younger than any of them. He had always been a man. Her man, and there was a time when Marcey thought of killing her own family whenever they spoke of sacrificing him. Hearing that someone less important was hurting someone she loved infuriated her. "Do we have her whereabouts?" Marcey asked.

A slight smile pierced across Hazik's lips. Out of habit, he pulled an ankle over his knee and started circling the small space between his shoe and pants leg. For anyone, obtaining federal information concerning informants was almost impossible, especially the important ones. However, the remedy was moving quickly, and Hazik was fast. His finger stopped trailing over his sock and just rested there. "I have everything you need. But use your training and remember which league this is."

Marcey knew he was referring to things she learned while training at the Federal Academy. Killing Kim was at the forefront of her mind, but since she was a federal witness who had already given a statement, death would not stop the jury from hearing her testimony, and the jury had the most sympathy as they listened to words from the dead. "We need her alive. If she is persuaded, the government will not risk a case of this magnitude based on doubt," she heard her uncle say, clarifying her thoughts.

"What if I can't persuade her?"

Delaying any response, she saw Hazik go inside his back pocket, pulling out a piece of folded paper. On there was the number to the man Hazik had been tailing Kim's every move. "The Feds will be moving her soon. Wait for the move, then go see her so that she knows we can reach her anywhere, and don't worry, Marcey, you're the best at getting what you want." winked Hazik as he got up to leave.

When Marcey closed the door behind her, she returned to her glass but did not take another sip. Hazik was right, she was the best at getting what she wanted, and she promised herself that for the sake of her son having his father, she would not fail.

$$\$\$\$$$

Her departure from Africa was only days behind Lil Ronnie and the kids, but call it a mother's tuition Lisa told Lonnie she wanted to make sure everyone had made it back safe and pulled off leaving him home. Since Lil Ronnie had moved her far away from Boynton, it took her half an hour to get there, but there was no fatigue. Pulling the kids' gifts out with her, Lisa rang the doorbell, feeling as happy as ever. Lisa was riding high on the best month of her life. Marrying Lil Ronnie's father with a wedding in one of her favorite countries and having her grandbabies present to witness topped anything, and only a bulldozer could take away her joy. Unfortunately, the loaded bulldozer was just on the other side of the door as it opened, and Lisa noticed distress plastering Tay's face. Walking the gifts over to the counter, Lisa immediately forgot all about her wedding in Africa. She turned back around to face Tay crossing her arms across her breast. "Where's Ronnie?" she asked.

The question sent a flash through Tay's eyes that Lisa picked up far before Tay could look away. It took a second for Tay to respond. "I don't know. Lil Ronnie left after we landed." she said, but the energy wasn't there.

Lisa's eyes slit, sensing bullshit. She looked on for a few seconds, then spoke a little bit more firmly. "Tay, you have never in your life lied to me, and I suggest you don't start now. Where is Lil Ronnie?"

"He didn't want me to say anything. You know how he is about you," she heard Tay say, and Lisa cursed in her voice.

All their life, she and her son had fought and figured out trouble together. Now, after he discovered she was battling HIV, the burden of his life, he tried to keep away from her. However, Lisa could see it on Tay's face that now was not one of those times. "Is he hurt?" she asked. Seeing her shake her head, Lisa accepted, with a breath of relief while thinking further. Not much trouble came their way. Threats in the streets were eliminated after Mike's death. Mercey's husband, who wanted to indict Lil Ronnie, had been murdered, so there wasn't much to go by until Lisa remembered the white woman Pawlowski coming to her home and harassing them.

"Shit" she said, jotting her eyes at Tay. "That bitch put my son in jail, didn't she?"

The accurate assumption blurred Tay's eyes, but her head started nodding feverishly. Tears exploded from her eyes, and Lisa grabbed her close, hugging her daughter-in-law.

"He'll be home. He'll be home," she said, counseling her also while sending out prayers from her heart.

This was another hurdle they'd clear. She was sure of it.

CHAPTER 2

Five days after Lil Ronnie turned himself in, Pawlowski put in an order to have Kim and her family moved further south, to a quiet cornerstone in Monroe County. The move took Kim's mother Jackie by surprise, and her six-year-old son had an all-out fit, realizing he was leaving Lil Ronnie and the others. It hurted Kim knowing Jay looked at Lil Ronnie like a father, and his kids were as close to Jay as she could have ever guessed. However, neither Jay nor her mother knew Lil Ronnie's capabilities. Remaining in the city at her mom's put them all in danger. Therefore, Kim moved them without any hesitance and tried her best to find comfort in the four-bedroom home.

Outside the home exterior was designed similarly to the other twenty or so homes on the street. All of them came with fluffy green grass, picket fences, with either a white or pink coating covering the homes. Kim looked up and down the street as she waited on the porch while Pawlowski's car to come to a stop. The neighborhood was not what she was used to. Everything was quiet without anyone hanging on the sidewalks. All the windows were covered tight, and as she recalled, she had not seen a single person coming or going. When Pawlowski got out, asking if she was okay, Kim seemed startled, forgetting just that fast that Pawlowski had joined her.

Kim informed her she was fine and then Pawlowski glanced at the house making small talk, "Do you like it?"

Turning toward her new home, Kim ran her fingers through her short-styled cut, thinking of the price she paid to live there. "It's nice. Quiet," Kim pointed out.

"Yes. We try to locate safe houses in the most discreet areas. This neighborhood is almost completely off the map," informed Pawlowski.

Looking at both ends of the street again, Kim thought of the conversation she and Pawlowski had on Pawlowski's way over. "Did you order security?"

"I did. "There'll be two vehicles, one to follow you and another to patrol the house at all times."

"I don't want them," Kim said. Referring to her security.

"But I thought you were comfortable having them around." Pawlowski stated, looking at her.

"I know what I said before," Kim said peeking at the house. When she looked back at Pawlowski, her voice carried certainty: "But this is what I want. You said yourself that Lil Ronnie will never know where I went, and honestly, while my mother is oblivious, I'd like to keep it that way for as long as I can.

"Precaution is what we're good at. Refusing puts you and your mother and your son at greater risk."

There was a pause with both women standing on the front lawn. Kim looked at the white agent, knowing she was the devil, but a devil who had given her an out. Taking a deep breath, Kim started walking toward the house. When she got to the door, she looked back, speaking one last time. "We made a deal so I can stay out here with my son, but we are not friends. Please make your visit as short as possible and do not have your men watch over me and my family."

Kim waited for Pawlowski to nod her head, then walked inside the house, locking the door behind her. Her back pressed against the door, and out of nowhere, she started weeping silently. How could she? Is what ran through her mind every time she had a second to herself. Li'l Ronnie had shown her everything. Gave her and her son everything. House, cars, and so much clothing that a lot of it had to be left behind, and despite his other women, he even gave her time. So much had transpired between them. Kim was sure dying for Lil Ronnie would be a gift of repayment, but she had fallen weak because of time. Feeling her legs getting weak, Kim slid to the floor, burying her face in her arms. ' There was no other way. It was either him or her child, which is what usually gave her strength to get past her thoughts; however, before she could come around and get back up, Jackie cleared her throat, snapping her back to the present.

"Kim, what is the matter?" Jackie asked, bending to help her up.

Taking her time, Kim hugged her mother to hide her expression while at the same time trying to regroup. "It's nothing, mother. I'm just thinking about a lot."

Feeling her mother's release, Kim looked up to see her mother frowning. "Now I don' let you move us out of the only city I know without fighting you. You're about to tell me what's going on."
"Momma don't-"
"Don't momma me shit!" snapped Jackie. "Why

are the damn police involved? What have you done?"

Badly Kim wanted to escape and run out the door like she was a child again, but her own child was upstairs, so she'd eventually have to come right back. Wiping her eyes, Kim thought of something to say. "I got into a little trouble, and Pawlowski is making sure it doesn't happen again."

Her words instantly bounced around in her mother's head, and mentally, Kim was already wincing at her mistake.

"The police don't help people like us." She heard her mother say soon as her words settled. "They help snitches and white folks, and I'm hoping like hell you ain't either!"

Hearing the truth, Kim felt tears flood her eyes. She burst into a loud shriek and ran and locking herself in the bathroom.

$$$

On the sixth floor of the Westside County Jail, Mel was lying back in his bunk when someone came running down the hall, yelling his name. "Aye, ya man, about to come over the catwalk!"

Lil Ronnie III

Spank, an inmate from Mel's neighborhood, said excitedly Swinging his legs from the bunk, all 300 and 6'0 plus frames stood. Mel walked out of the cell quickly to get over near the window to view his man, and just as he got there, Lil Ronnie's wild fro was the first thing he saw coming over the hill. Handcuffed behind his back, he watched two FBI agents guide him over the walk. In silence, Mel stood there, thinking of his man's fall while watching him at the same time. Fighting his own case for months, he never once let it get to him. Mel moved around the county jail at will, and everyone respected both his size and his ability to get down. However, as soon as Ja'nell came to visit, informing him of Lil Ronnie's arrest, the shit tore him apart. The indictment made everything Mel was in jail for pointless. They were who they were, and all of Lil Ronnie's hard work went for nothing, and he felt he would be nothing if he didn't sacrifice and kill Blake the way he had.

Since the catwalk was only a couple steps into their view, Lil Ronnie vanished from his sights in no time, but Mel continued standing there, looking at the last spot Lil Ronnie had appeared. The guy who had come and got him must have been keeping track of time because soon after he walked over, peeking out the narrow plexiglass of a window.

"Shit fucked up homie, I can't believe both of you niggas are in jail."

Spank was the guy's name, and Mel looked at him with a glance that made him timid. "Yeah, I know," Mel finally said, shaking his head. "All this shit seems to be happening so fast, but my nigga gonna' Casanova this bitch."

"Anything you need me to do?" Spank asked.

"Yeah, try to get my man up here, and if that don't work, set him straight. Get him whatever the fuck he needs." Mel told him, then left to go back to his room.

$$$

The call came to Marcey as soon as she stepped out of the shower. She went over to her phone, spoke with the tail, and jotted down Kim's new address. There was no need to rush things; however, Marcey knew that each day, Lil Ronnie sat in jail tortured them both. Her more mental than anything but for him she knew hurt came to him financially as well as spiritually since he was as strongly family oriented as she was. Therefore, she planned to be at the address first thing in the morning.

In the meantime, she needed to tend to other business. Business that she was now starting to regret due to a guilt consciousness she was building on behalf of Lil Ronnie. Going over to her closet Marcey slipped into one of the dresses hanging inside, pulled out a pair of matching heels followed by her purse. After grabbing her keys, she made a stop in the hall where boxes meant for Lil Ronnie were and opened one taking out ten kilos. Sticking them in a shopping bag Marcey locked up her house and headed to the hotel her and Spazz kept for their rendezvous. When she got there, Spazz tried greeting her with a kiss, but Marcey moved past him bluntly.

"Here's the ten Derek wanted, did he give you, my money?" Marcey asked.

"Yeah" he pointed at the bed. "But why the fuck you putting me in the middle of that. Business is between you two, I'm just ya fuck buddy, remember that?"

"Well, this is how shit is going to be until I figure out Derek's role in all this." Stated Marcey as she watched Spazz face bawl into a scowl.

"Fuck is you talking about?" He asked.

Walking over to the bed Marcey unzipped the bag holding her money. "Derek's cousin is a rat. She just got Lil Ronnie indicted and until I know rather, he's involved or not his business goes directly through you." She said and looked up just in time to see Spazz getting ready to protest. "It's either that or I cut it off here and now."

"Hol' up, you come in this muthafucka acting different because that nigga got knocked. You know Derek ain't got shit to do with that. Lil Ronnie fall is his own." She heard Spazz say. Marcey gave notice to his words ringing true Marcey hiding her smile from his stirring aggression. After all, Spazz and Derek was only given the chance due to Spazz sexy aggressiveness. He was slim with a lion endowed over and below the waist. Marcey had fallen instantly. Almost like she had with Lil Ronnie but differently. Whereas Lil Ronnie captured her heart both voluntarily and involuntarily. Spazz was like a flame that she couldn't tell would sizzle out or flare widely. Marcey went quiet for a second using the distraction of the money to smother her smile but after it was zipped back up her beautiful lips went along displaying their perfection. "I'm taking that as an, okay?" She smiled businesslike before pointing at the kilos she dropped off.

Watching his pissed expression remain silent Marcey lifted the bag on her shoulder and tried walking past him.

"Cool but since we're changing shit up Derek and I decided we're expanding toward Boynton. The park is for the taken."

Marcey feet stopped the second his words came out. She looked at him as if he'd lost half of his brain. "I specifically told Derek long as I'm providing him, he can never sell in this city." She said whirling back around to face him.

"No, you said he can never sell in the same city as Lil Ronnie. That nigga's in jail now ain't no reason not to."

Marcey eyes glared but the look on Spazz face told her he didn't give a fuck. She took a deep breath before shaking her head in frustration.

"It's gone come a time you have to pick." He said holding her eye contact. Marcey saw him walking over to her towering her so closely pieces of his dreadlocks brushed against her shoulders. "And on everything I love Marcey it better be me." He said in a tone that would have made the average girl cringe but while looking up at him Marcey knew there was no competition. Lil Ronnie was Lil Ronnie. Her Ronnie. The father of her child and till this day she still hoped he would give up the other women to have her. "What makes you think I will?" She asked Spazz, holding her stance with the bag still resting on her arm.

The diamonds engraved in Spazz teeth glittered at her and before Marcey knew what happened Spazz have shoved her against the wall ripping off her clothes. Her breast was exposed first, and she felt his mouth sucking on them. Then his hands went under her dress snatching her panties so hard her body jerked as he ripped them. The roughness turned her on and by the time Spazz dick was out she was bent over ready for him to fuck her.

"You're telling me you won't?" Marcey heard him growl near her ear just as his dick slid inside her pussy.

His stroke made her gasp. Marcey reached her hands out to the door for leverage holding herself upright as he stroked her again. His question played in her head. Battling with him actually considering she would choose him. That was until her moans interfered with her thoughts. Spazz fingers sunk hard into her skin, and she could feel his testicles slamming against her thighs each time he pulled her waist into him. There bent over behind the hotel's room door Marcey felt convulsions after each climax he pulled from her body. When her moaning subsided, she felt thick liquid of Spazz semen ozz out of her trailing down her leg but was too afloat to think of any possibilities.

"Get me a fucking towel." She told Spazz before redirecting herself to the hotel's bed.

CHAPTER 3

The next morning Marcry left Spazz in bed, stopped by the house to drop off the money then headed south. It was just approaching 9a.m. by the time she arrived in Monroe pulling behind the tail. Watching as the older gentleman prop himself high in the passenger seat Marcey listened to him narrate how the Federal protective security was surprisingly poor. Pawlowski had to give Kim a lot of leniencies because for a 5k1 witness protection was usually a lot tighter. As he explained Marcey scanned up and down the street at parked cars who could have been undercover. When she was certain the man surveillance was accurate, she thanked him. Watched him get into his minivan and pull away then drove off herself headed straight for the house.

$$$

Going inside the kitchen to fix a pot of coffee Jackie thoughts were still on her daughter. She didn't know what but felt whatever Kim was in was messy. Witness protection was for those in hiding. Were they hiding? Jackie thought as she got ready to take the pot down from the cabinet. The car pulling into their drive made her pull her arms down and Jackie walked to the window for a closer look. Her first thought was another cop coming to check on her daughter, but something told her whoever was inside didn't own a badge. A top designer heel stepping on the pavement was the first thing Jackie saw before Marcey entire body appeared holding a tote bag. Having no clue who the woman was Jackie left the kitchen meeting Marcey at the door.

"Yes, how can I help you?" Jackie asked with the door partly opened.

Marcey smiled, giving Jackie nothing less than a professional approach. "Hi, I'm Marcey, is your daughter here? I really need to speak to her."

"Are you the police?" Jackie asked ready to send them away.

Noticing Marcey gushed. "No ma'am, complete opposite. I'm here to see if I can change her mind. She's making a mistake." Marcey truthfully said, keeping up the soft smile and friendly glare.

"Is Lil Ronnie involved in all this?" Jackie asked.

Seeing Marcey head confirming the worse Jackie head fell in shame. When she looked back up, she asked, "Can you fill me in before I go and get my daughter?" After Marcey agreed Jackie let Marcey in escorting her to a living room chair.

Jackie listened to Marcey speak for several minutes while replaying Kim sudden move back to her apartment. Feeling every bit of it was true, Jackie jumped up in the middle of the conversation racing upstairs. She and Kim went back and forth for several minutes before Jackie had her daughter by the wrist dragging her downstairs.

Marcey looked at the pajamas hugging Kim body and wanted to strangle her with its every thread. Trash! Is what shouted off in Marcey head but it's what she thought of all Lil Ronnie extra women. She stood as mother and daughter reached the living room however the cordial vibe was no longer present. Her eyes were already on Kim but when Kim found hers it was like the eve of hell breaking.

"What! What do you want!!" Kim screamed at the top of her lungs. Mad, her mother not only pulled her downstairs, but also had let Marcey in.

"I told you what she wanted, and you will sit down and listen!" Her mother screamed for Marcey shoving Kim toward a seat. Marcey sat after Kim then Jackie, however her unity was not mistaken as she sat very close to her daughter protectively. Putting her glaze on Marcey Jackie told her to share what she had.

"We need you to change your statement." Marcey stated bluntly.

"I can't." Kim spats right back without looking at her mother nor Marcey.

"Kim, how do you think Lil Ronnie is feeling right now getting buried in a fucking cage because of your mistake?"

"I had no choice. They were going to take me from my child and that's something Lil Ronnie gon' have to understand," Kim said.

"You knew the risk and had plenty of chances to step away from it. Instead, you go against Lil Ronnie word and sell shit on your own."

As if Marcey words were causing her head to spin Kim buried her face in her hands. Jackie pulled her daughter under her arm holding her while her and Marcey listened to Kim tears. It was evident Kim had dug up something without knowing what came with it. She wasn't a kid with boyfriends. No. She was a woman stuck in the field of a big-time drug dealer with murderous friends. Jackie knew the image was appealing but when shit hits the fan only the right woman could stand under it.

Taking a deep breath Jackie continued hugging her daughter while asking, "Kim Jackie needs to know what you are going to do."

Seconds passed then out of nowhere Kim sprouted to her feet. "Get out! Get the fuck out of this house right now!! Her finger was pointed toward the front door, but Jackie didn't budge. She was there to save Lil Ronnie freedom and giving up was not who she was. "Was this always a part of your plan. To cross Lil Ronnie if things got heated. He needs you Kim, the same way you needed him when you and your child had no help."

"Lil Ronnie done this to himself. He killed people. Killed my baby father and if he hadn't neither of us would be in this position."

"And your baby father helped kill people he loved but that is not the point." Jackie stated. Grabbing the tote bag, she came in with Jackie unzipped it showing its contents. "There's two-hundred and fifty thousand in here, take it and do whatever we're asking you to do."

Jackie and Kim both looked at all the neatly wrapped bundles inside the bag, however Jackie saw Kim shaking her head. "I can't. What's done is done, they will prosecute him anyway."

"The feds can do nothing without you and they're not going to risk it without your cooperation." Jackie saw Kim fall back in her seat and sensing she was close Jackie tossed the bag at their feet while continuing to speak. "I know your son is your top priority but don't forget the good Lil Ronnie has done for the both of you. He could have killed you the night Jay was murdered, don't let him regret that." Jackie stood and asked Kim for her answer herself. When weeping became the only reply Marcey asked Jackie to walk her out and headed for her car. By the time she got to her car Jackie was looking both angered and confused.

"Ma'am please take this with kindness. Lil Ronnie is connected to some enormously powerful people who found this address with nothing more than a call. Kim will not be safe no matter where she goes, so make her take the money, it's best."

"She's scared." Jackie said, regarding her daughter.

"And so is Lil Ronnie but I am standing here for everyone's future."

"Is she really in danger?" Jackie asked.

"Not from Lil Ronnie. He'd never touch her, but there are people over him calling the shots, and those people do not care about human life."

"If she changes her story, what will the feds do?" Jackie asked.

"She's going to jail. Marcey said, But not for long, and definitely not as long as Lil Ronnie would be." Opening her car door, Marcey added, "I'm willing to put more money aside for the security of her child when she's away. That's half a million dollars." Marcey said, handing Jackie a number to reach her.

Nodding Jackie watched Marcey get inside the car and pull off. She walked back inside, thinking of Lil Ronnie. She didn't know him much but had seen what he'd done to her daughter and grandson's lifestyle. Despite what it took to get there, he took care of them like he loved them. Kim was back upstairs in her room crying when Jackie made it back into the house. Going to her, Jackie had a mother-daughter talk. It took a lot of explaining, but eventually Jackie made her daughter see the future.

"I'm going to call Marcey, let her know you're not cooperating with the feds any longer. Do you mind?" Jackie asked.

When Kim shook her head for her to call Marcey, Jackie left, proud that her daughter was doing the right thing.

$$$

After the arraignment, Lil Ronnie was returned to solitary confinement, where he was kept housed away from the population. His face was on every local news station in the state, and deputies feared his popularity would incite leadership. When the steel door closed behind him, Lil Ronnie sat on his bunk, trying his best to keep from stressing. He thought of Kim's betrayal. The fact that he couldn't reach her. He knew Hazik would keep his word and turn every rock to free him, but would it be enough. Having little faith, Lil Ronnie grew frustrated and slung the stacks of papers on his bed to the floor. His anger pushed his thoughts to the creator of his situation, and he thought of Zay setting up Kim in the first place. Needing to relieve some of the pressure he had built, Lil Ronnie leaned against the concrete wall behind him and put his focus entirely on Zay.

$$$

"Mission completed, said Marcey soon as she walked inside the jewelry store, finding Hazik over a tray of diamonds.

Stopping himself from examining the stones, Hazik put down the tiny magnifying glass and came from behind the counter. "Wonderful" he beamed, extending his arms for a hug. When Marcey fell into his embrace, he asked, Was it a task?"

"Besides fighting urges to kill her, no. The mother made her come to terms." Releasing herself from his arms, Marcey walked to the counter, looking at the diamonds. "Are these from home?" She asked.

"Yes, and I'm sick of it." Hazik complained. "The son of a bitch sends every piece of crap he digs, including cement."

Seeing exactly what he was talking about, Jackie

laughed. "Tell him to stop, why don't you?"

"Because the fucker gets lucky at times." Hazik informed, making Marcey laugh more. Picking up the magnifying glass, he got back to work but continued talking. "Have you been to see Lil Ronnie yet?"

"No, Marcey answered.

"Why? You know he's going to be pissed about that."

"Uncle, we spoke of this when you were at the condo."

"Yes, but I didn't get into your business then. I am now," Hazik said, seriously loving the two together.

"Lil Ronnie is not ready to settle down. If India were still alive, I'd be the fourth baby momma, and Lil Ronnie is pressed about keeping us all Marcey said sadly.

"Most of his women you knew of before you two got together. You can't expect him to change."

"I deserve it." Marcey replied.

"I'm sure you are, but that is what you chose." Putting the magnifying glass back down, Hazik looked at his niece closely. "What are you doing now?" He asked.

Looking away from him at the stones, Marcey thought of lying, but considered she had done enough of that with her and Lil Ronnie's relationship already. "I'm seeing someone." She admitted seeing color drain from his face immediately.

"Who?" He asked.

"Someone from a different city. I know what I'm doing, Uncle."

Not liking what he was hearing, Hazik felt an instant ache to his bones. "Blood will pour the minute Lil Ronnie finds out, and that blood will be on your hands, is that what you want?"

Unable to reply, Marcey just stood there, staring through the stones. Lil Ronnie would be sure to do exactly what Hazik said, but she didn't need to feel any more guilt than she was already feeling. Clearing her throat, Marcey came from her daze. "No matter if I remain single or sleep with anyone else, I'm not taking Lil Ronnie back until he chooses only me."

"Does this have anything to do with your mother?" Hazik asked, and the question gave Marcey pause.

Her first response was no, because she had not

thought of her mother and father in years. Her remembrance of them was very shallow, and the little she did keep with her was not for conversational purposes. But now that Hazik had mentioned it the resemblance was starting to feel familiar.

One of the last things she could remember about her parents' togetherness was the arguments between her father's cheating and her mother's complaints. The disputes were so frequent that neither of them had little time for her. Being drugged from house to house during separations made her unstable, and for the longest time, loving another human was not for Marcey. However, as soon as she realized love was in her and for Lil Ronnie, she wanted to clutch on to it and be everything her parents were not. "Now that I think of it, it's possible. I could never respect Poppa because he tore our family down, so maybe I'm afraid," Marcey informed.

Showing a supportive smile, Hazik hugged his niece one last time. "Don't let fear stop what you and Lil Ronnie have together. Accept what you can and don't let him find out about your extra dealings." Warning her once more to go and see Lil Ronnie Hazik walked his niece out, but there was one thing nagging at him, and it had been for some time. "Now that your relationship with Lil Ronnie is in the light, are you ready to confess to Bell's death?"

Crinkling her brows Marcey replied, are you insinuating I know what happened in Bell's death?"

"You're highly intelligent. Who met a young boy far more closer to your age than Bell and one who had all the correct tools. So yes, I guess I am."

"Lil Ronnie wouldn't kill Bell, not for me or money, because Bell had gained his respect."

"So, you pulled the trigger?" Hazik smirked.

Time passed as Marcey stood at the store's door. The perfect lines of her brows were still crinkled, as she mulled over her uncle's question. Then her brows relaxed. "I'll go see Lil Ronnie if you need me to; other than that, he can wait until he gets home."

Chuckling Hazik closed the door behind her, happy he had a thoroughbred as a niece.

CHAPTER 4

"The voicemail you are trying to reach has not been set up yet. Please hang up and try your call again." Taking the phone from her ear, Pawlowski waited a few more minutes before trying again.

"Maybe she's busy, Pawlowski told herself after another call to Kim went straight to her voicemail. Noting the time Pawlowski moved on, diving back into her case work. The evidence Selvester had on the case left piles of paperwork she needed to organize in case Lil Ronnie decided to go to trial. Starting by date, Pawlowski almost felt like she was wasting time as she realized each piece of paper, she touched had little or no evidence of Lil Ronnie. He was almost a ghost in theory, but she had all the physical evidence she needed; therefore, when her boss knocked on the door, interrupting her, her face was a confident smile.

"Pawlowski, how's it going?" he asked, taking a seat.

It's moving along well. Harrison doesn't stand a chance," she said before asking, "Is there anything I can do for you?"

"As a matter of fact, there is. This case has become somewhat of an attention grabber. Even though the media is getting involved, I don't want you letting this case get away from you.

Pawlowski forced a broader smile while stenciling her fingers together. "Trust me, Slate, there is no chance. I have enough evidence to bury him," she stated.

"Honored to hear that, but for extra measures, I'll be more hands on as well, kind of like the presence I showed during Kimberly's interview."

Deflation swirled up her throat, but Pawlowski held within her confidence. "Slate, I've worked this case harder than any. My rank alone should show you I'm more than capable."

"Are we really going there?" Challenged Slate almost as fast as the words came from her mouth.

Slate was one of the men who'd powered his way through the channels just as Selvester had. Like every man had, but unfortunately for her, he was not the type to loosen his tie and say, fuck me for a position. No Slate was by the book, and nowhere in the rules suggested her breast size as an exception.

"No, Slate, you're more than welcome to join."

"Then that's good, you wouldn't mind running some of it by me." Pawlowski heard him say.

Taking a deep breath, she said, "Your timing could not have been better. This is Mr. Harrison's file, and as you can see, it's thick." She tried sliding it to him, but once the papers were on his side of the desk, Slate just stared at them.

"I rather you walk me through it, he replied instead.

Offended, Pawlowski pulled the stack back and forced another smile. "Sure, no problem," she said, clearing her throat. "Uhm, for starters, we're going with the two murders, and the murder of Bernard is still pending. We are just waiting for a glimpse of connection. Then we have the drugs, and from what we've learned between Bernard, Xavier and Kimberly, the kilos are close to triple digits."

"Are the drugs inside the indictment?" Slate asked.

"We're pushing to supersede."

"Another indictment?" he asked.

"Yes," nodded Pawlowski.

"Pawlowski, just how much physical evidence do we have?"

Feeling her skin flush, Pawlowski was starting to sense Slate's aggravation. "There were drugs found during the raid."

"Drugs Kimberly sold."

"Yes. Lil Ronnie drugs."

"Which was left undocumented since she's your star witness." Slate's chest rose under his tailored suit, taking a deep breath. After he exhaled, his chubby cheeks seemed to hang lower. "Pawlowski, what I'm hearing is you have nothing except Kimberly, and although she is creditable, you can't change a case based solely on her. I thought there was more evidence than this."

"Kimberly and I have an understanding. She's more ready than we are."

Nodding, Slate took her word but asked, "Have you been in contact with her?"

"Actually, I spoke to her just before you stepped in." Pawlowski lied. "We'll speak again later."

Rising from her office chair, Slate adjusted his suit coat and cleared his throat again. "There will be no room for fucking up. Make sure your witness is ready because I'd hate to intervene a second time."

"Likewise," retorted Pawlowski, grateful once Slate was out of her office. Closing her office door, Pawlowski made it back to her desk, snatching up her phone. Back-to-back, she continued getting the voicemail and eventually grabbed her bags in frustration. This would be an hour and a half trip Kim was making her take, but after the conversation with Slate Pawlowski, felt it was worth it.

$$$

The bundles of cash were still in the same spot that Jackie had left it. Days had passed since Kim walked by it. She knew her cleanliness mother had left it there on purpose. Reminding her of another attachment to doing what everyone but the authorities knew was right. Kim herself left it there because the money was the last of her worries. It wasn't about the money, but the things Marcey and her mother had said. Lil Ronnie had given her life by not taking hers and given her life again after putting her and her child in a home without taking care of finances. She was happy there—actually, happier than her and her baby father's relationship had ever been—and the price she was making Lil Ronnie pay for it was jail by her own tongue. Her confession, the one Slate made her confess to, ran through her head so much it hurt, and up until Jackie visited, Kim really did believe everything she had said in the interview room couldn't be undone. At least that is what Pawlowski made her believe, but Pawlowski was wrong.

The ring tone on her phone rang for the umpteenth time, and had it not been for her mother bringing it downstairs, Kim would have kept it buried beneath her pillow. "You're going to have to tell them eventually." Her mother said, holding the phone out to her. Taking it, Kim tossed it on the sofa, not yet ready to face Pawlowski.

"Lil Ronnie will never accept me again, Kim said, pacing.

She watched her mother take a seat near the money and pull it onto her lap. "Lil Ronnie's only concern is going free, and even if that is true, you have enough money to start your life over."

Glancing at the money in Jackie's hand, Kim shook her head. "I was never with Lil Ronnie for his money. Maybe at first, but who he is to Jay and what he was to me outgrew anything. I'm going to jail once Pawlowski finds out I am no longer cooperating, and I don't want Lil Ronnie or anyone thinking I stopped for his money."

"So what are you saying?" She heard her mother ask before adding, "Kim, we're not giving this money back." The look her mother gave with the statement almost forced Kim to laugh, but before her mind could get too far away, her cell phone rang again; however, this time as soon as it stopped, a familiar banging came on the door. Kim looked at her mother, who looked at her. Taking a deep breath, Kim said, "Fuck it!"

$$$

"I lied! Everything I told you was a lie!!" Kim

shouted soon as she saw Pawlowski phony face getting ready to smile. Caught off guard, Pawlowski stood there with her mouth agape and speechless. "I don't know anything about any murders, and I sold my own drugs." Kim continued to rant.

The fine lashes on Pawlowski's lids took several fast blinks before she was seen pulling at the helms of her suit jacket. Swallowing the lump that had suddenly formed in her throat, Pawlowski shook her baffled expression. "Mind if I come in?" she politely asked.

Knowing she had no choice; Kim left the door open and went into the dining area. It was all Pawlowski needed to regroup as her steps grew hot on Kim's tail. "What the hell happened?" Grilled Pawlowski barely giving Kim space to sit.

"Nothing happened. I just can't live with myself telling all of these lies."

"You mean covering up lies. Don't you start this hood guilt trip shit on me. We had a deal, Kimberly!" Pawlowski snapped with her boss's words still fresh in her head.

"A deal you forced on me, and that's what I'll tell the jury." Kim snapped back, causing Pawlowski to step so far up in her face that the two nearly kissed.

"You better watch your mouth before I lock your ass up right this second, Pawlowski shouted, meaning every word. "Your freedom, your child, all of it will go away at the snap of my finger, Do I make myself clear?" Taking her silence as agreement, Pawlowski calmed down and tried using her training to manipulate Kim. "Have you been in contact with Lil Ronnie? If so, I can have him under more charges." Taking a deep breath, Pawlowski said, "We're on the same team, Kimberly, and the only ones who care for you are the people in this house."

Tears crowded her eyes, but Kim was over the threats from Pawlowski. "Lil Ronnie hasn't contacted me and he didn't do anything." She said, jerking her body backwards in the chair in order to dodge the hand Pawlowski slammed on the table.

"So you are ready to go to prison! Is that it, Kimberly?"

"Get out of my face!" Kim shouted back, jumping up and knocking the dining chair over. "You can do whatever you have to do, but I'm not lying for you any longer!"

Their voices had risen so high, Jackie rushed down the stairs to get between them. 'Street heard my daughter from upstairs, and then you did as well. It's time for you to leave, Officer," Jackie stated, putting herself toe-to-toe with Pawlowski.

"Your daughter's decision will put her in prison for a very long time. Is that what you guys want?"

"What we want is for you to leave. If her decision

changes, you'll know."

Cutting her eyes at Kim Pawlowski, wanted to do just as Jackie wanted. Kill her, strangle her. Do something that would prevent her from looking foolish in Slate's face, however, Pawlowski felt her best and her only hope was to pray Kim got back on their train. Flushing the anger from her face, Pawlowski backed away, but not before saying her last words. "Thank your mother; you're not in cuffs right now. I'm giving you one week to start making sense again, then I'm pulling the cord.

CHAPTER 5

Big Blue sat behind the tinted windows of his Excursions watching the taillights of Tay car leave his street. When it finally made a turn, he continued looking in a daze, thinking of the words Lil Ronnie sent her to deliver. "Your people must go."

"Who?" He asked.

"Zay and Lil Ronnie said you must do it soon as possible."

The conversation lasted less than a minute and, in the end, Big Blue could truly say he didn't know what made Lil Ronnie send an order for him to take the life of a lifelong friend, but for good reason he had agreed.

"Dammit!" The words flew from his mouth knowing Zay had fucked up by being a rat. When he grew tired of looking down the street one of his hands tightened around the steering wheel while the other started the ignition. Zay's home was only a couple of streets over and by the time he made it on the street Veronica, Zay's wife was just about to get inside her car. BigBlue watched the young girl climb inside wearing a pair of skintight jeans that showed her ass and made him reach beside where he had his revolver laying grabbing his crotch. For as long as he knew Veronica, he wanted her and at times BigBlue thought she'd put herself in his path, but certain lines were never crossed.

He slowed enough to let her leave without noticing him then pulled into the yard honking his horn like he always did. In seconds Zay head popped out but there were no smiles. Shit had gotten rough over the past year. Their once airtight crew had fallen to shreds, but Blake's murder had brought the two of them at odds making Zay and the others feel like he had taken sides with Lil Ronnie. Refusing to argue who was right, Big Blue lifted his big body half out the driver's window like everything was cool.

"You feel like moving? I need you to ride with me," said Big Blue, knowing Zay wouldn't turn him down.

It only took a few seconds for him to decide before BigBlue had him in the Excursions. "Where the move at?" asked Zay, leaning the passenger seat all the way back to get comfortable.

"Just outside the city, dropping the last few of those things off." Said BigBlue pointing toward the back at an empty gym bag.

As they drove, all Big Blue could think about was how Zay had turned fed. *First Blake, now Zay* he thought with embarrassment. "You still on that helping the law shit?" Big Blue asked and as if Zay knew the topic would be reinvited, he exhaled before speaking.

"Look man, this shit isn't about no street moral shit. We knew Blake all our lives, and you were just gonna let Lil Ronnie get away with murdering him."

"Blake got what he got because he's doing the same shit as you. The kid warned him. I warned him."

"Fuck that. Lil Ronnie ain't walking these streets ever again."

Inside the dark interior of his truck Big Blue shook his head. It was the same words he'd gotten when he first asked Zay if he was behind setting Kim up. Almost as if snitching was a form of bravado, Big Blue regretted not killing his friend that day.

A pack of Newport's came out of Zay pocket and Big Blue didn't say anything as Zay fired it up. The smoke simmered and swirled around as Big Blue drove headed straight for Beeline Road. "For over twenty years, we have been hustling together. Sold more than any man in the city... Shit it was our city." Zay said in the middle of his puffs. "Now this lil muthafucka come and think he can do whatever. He's a punk with a plug Blue and soon you gone realize that."

His words were a distance as Big Blue continued driving, listening and becoming angrier on the inside. However, to keep Zay off guard he said, "My main thing has always been to keep us on point. We could have gotten revenge on Lil Ronnie multiple ways, but not one that made the very streets we were raised on shame us. Ain't no forgiveness in snitching." When the Excursion turned down Beeline's dark road Big Blue could feel his palms begin sweating. The hand closer to the door slid out of view for a second getting a grip on his gun.

"Yeah, well it's a good thing I ain't looking for forgiveness." Zay retorted without a pinch of remorse.

They went further down the road and Big Blue was finally able to say what he really wanted. "You's a stupid muthafucka. You really think Lil Ronnie gone let you set him and his girl up without reprisal?" Big Blue said while veering off to the side of the road.

Zay went to lean up and say something slick but locked eyes on the hate plastering Big Blue's face. Before he could react to what he knew was coming Big Blue arm rose firing right into his chest.

"See what the fuck you got me out here doing!" Bam! He shot Zay again. This time closer to the stomach. When he heard Zay wheezing trying to catch his breath Big Blue jumped out of the truck pulling Zay on side of the road. The street was so dark he couldn't even see his face, but Zay silhouette guided Big Blue aim as his revolver released four more shots. All of them tore into Zay face and by the time Big Blue pulled off he was sure if the bullets didn't kill Zay in time the wild animals surely would.

$$\$\$\$$$

Discovering Kim was wavering toward recanting her statement made Pawlowski return to her office closing herself in. In the chair behind her desk, she sat in complete darkness fuming over their conversation. There was no doubt in her mind someone had gotten to Kim. And to think she was actually about to nail Lil Ronnie was a joke Pawlowski could drink to. But there were no beverages inside her office, only files stenciled with Lil Ronnie's name. Feeling depleted, Pawlowski had the urge to toss every piece of paper with the name Ronnie Harrison on it out of her office but couldn't force herself to move. Instead, she sat there through the night dosing occasionally until daylight seeped through the office. When she stood to fix her a pot of coffee Pawlowski thought of the small area Lil Ronnie was from and the respect he had there. Everyone seemed to love the kid. Everyone except the law and people he'd harmed. People he'd harmed! Pawlowski last words echoed back in her head and with them was a thought.

Going to her computer Pawlowski looked for the very first thing that made her drown Lil Ronnie. It was the day three women and one male who she later learned most of them were connected, had been savagely killed in four different locations. One that caught her interest in particular was the mother of Lil Ronnie first born, India Harrison. The murdered victim had been shot multiple times on the side of the street where cookouts ran by Lil Ronnie was being held. Pawlowski had spoken to the victim's parents several times before and both seemed helpless. However, only one of the parents seemed devastated and they couldn't be of help but promised she had their support.

Going to the contact information Pawlowski wrote down the address and left, hoping the husband was as desperate as she had beckoned. Calling before arriving, she could see Karen watching through a living room window, but several run ins told Pawlowski the woman did not care for her. Ringing the doorbell, Pawlowski used her knuckles to knock loud enough for Lance to hear and became relieved by his greeting.

"Hello Agent Pawlowski, I'm glad you called." He smiled before waving her inside. By the time the door closed Karen was standing beside her husband with an entirely different look. "What are you coming here for?" Karen asked. Her face just as bitter as her words.

To not make her own self seem bitter Pawlowski put on her smile but directed her attention to the person she came to see. "There was a setback in the case and I'm hoping one of you remembered anything that can put it back on track." She told Lance.

"Gssh, I'm sorry to hear that. Here come into the living room and have a seat." Lance tried to guide her but Pawlowski politely refused.

"I'm pressed for time but if we can speak in private for a moment that would be nice." She said but the drawback on both husband-and-wife face answered before either of them could.

"Private" Lance uttered. 'That isn't necessary. My wife and I may have our differences of opinion but are on the same team." Lance could have said more but Pawlowski put up her hands stopping him.

"Okay. I just, what I'm about to say can rub a Peron wrong if they're not totally committed." Assuring her they were Pawlowski got down to it. "For the record I'm here because you said if I ever needed anything concerning the case all I had to do was ask."

Remembering what he had said Lance nodded, confirming, "And nothing has changed."

"Good because Lil Ronnie may be going free soon."

"That's impossible. He was just arrested!" Lance Exclaimed.

"I know, and I hate it as well, but there is nothing I can do. These kinds of things happen when people don't come forward or stick to their story."

Pawlowski saw Lance step away from his wife in a need to start pacing. She could tell as Karen stood there with her face baffled that they both wanted justice, but Karen anger was nowhere near her husband's. As Lance paced, he began taking deep breaths.

"That girl Kimberly, she was going to testify, what happened?" Karen asked.

"Witness become ashamed as the case grow old. She's threatened to recant her statement and I can't risk this case solely on her." Pawlowski looked over at Lance who was still pacing, saying, "Lil Ronnie is somebody to these people but they're forgetting the others who are getting hurt by his actions. I just want justice for your daughter and closure for you two."

Lance feet turned back toward them and on his face was a ball of anger. "Just tell me what I need to do."

"Are you sure?" Pawlowski asked, feeling her own heart accelerate. She watched Lance for a moment as his eyes grew crimson by the second.

"Long as it brings that murdering dope dealing son of a bitch down, I'll do it."

Unsure of his wife Pawlowski checked Karen by catching her eye contact but Karen expression was more dead than alive. However, time was closing and she needed to know who was on board. without further delay Pawlowski unveiled. "It could help the case if you testified. Specifically, something that tells the jury you were there and watched Lil Ronnie involvement in your daughter killing."

Lance thought hard and his nodding head was a sign to say he was close to denying any such remembrance but before words came out Pawlowski stopped him making herself clearer. "I don't care if you actually saw him or not. This is what we need in order to find him guilty."

"But what do I say if I don't know anything? Lying under oath is against the law." Lance said.

Pawlowski smirked with a thought to lash out at him. She was blatantly screaming, "fuck the law" right there under their roof in their faces for their daughter, but perplexed situations could make the smartest person naive. Maintaining her composure, she said, "Well first I'm here to represent the people therefore the law is in our favour. We have nothing to worry about and if you wish to proceed, I'll be glad to take my seat and explain everything that needs to be done."

At first Lance expression brought her worry. He stared at her then peeked in the direction of his wife before saying, "Sure, I understand. Have a seat and let's proceed."

After taking her seat, Pawlowski noticed the only one who remained standing was Karen. Pawlowski watched Karen tightly folded arms tensing under each other and was about to question her. However, before she could Karen turned and stormed off toward the back. "Will she be okay?" Pawlowski asked Lance.

"Hopefully yes. Karen believed India died from loving who she loved, and Lil Ronnie shouldn't be hated for loving her back."

"Love isn't supposed to get you killed." Informed Pawlowski.

Lance looked down the hall where Karen stormed off, they could hear her weeping. Moisture drenched his eyes causing him to take a deep breath. "Let's get this over with," he finally said.

An hour later Pawlowski felt relief as she gathered her bag and notes ready to leave. As soon as she stood her and Lance both eyes jolted toward a door slamming against the wall followed by Karen steam walking with her keys and purse in hand. Getting out of the way, as Lance tried to cut into his wife's path she heard. "Stay the hell away from me. You two are worse than any name who've mentioned in this house and I'm through with it all. The door slammed leaving Pawlowski unsure rather to stay and sooth Lance baffled look or leave behind Karen and give him time to himself. Deciding to go she rubbed his arm in sympathy then walked to the door.

"We'll stay in close contact and no matter what just know you're doing the right thing, Lance.

$$$

It had been a while since Derek last showed his face in the city. He had no real reason to until now. Knowing Lil Ronnie was locked up and the streets were for the taken he walked back and forth around the kitchen preparing everything he'd need to cover the park. Behind him Eyanna eyes followed his trail along with her words.

"I don't know much about this business, but it seemed safer with you in Delray." Eyanna said watching him remove a pot setting it on the counter, only for them both to repeat his steps. "The guy Lil Ronnie has only been locked up a week, even his men will get offended."

"Eyanna, this ain't Lil Ronnie city. I been away out of respect but before someone else takes claim of a park. I put an image on, I'll reclaim myself." He said knowing Eyanna knew little about the hustle.

"You've told me stories. The parks are his rather he's free or not."

"10th park is his. The east side has always belonged to Mel and myself, besides he'll be busy when he comes home."

"And what is that supposed to mean?" She asked.

Derek moved to pour water from one of the pots and through his side eye he saw her discomfort. Being one to reason with almost anyone Derek stopped what he was doing and placed all his attention on her. "Tell you what if the park ain't how I left it, then I'll leave it alone. But we're not switching anything out of fear, you understand me?" me said, keeping Spazz plan to himself.

Getting her to agree Derek kissed her on the lips then got back to work. Soon as the work was rocked and ready, he hit up Spazz telling him to put the extra men they had brought with them on post. When he pulled up at the east side park, not only was it as he left it, but the place seemed to be swarmed with just the right kind of company. Derek got out of the truck with a serious frown. From now on shit was going to be business pure and simple.

"Let's set this muthafucka off!" He said to Spazz when they met up and before long, he was at his best, braking orders and clocking workers.

$$$

Detective Greene case was moving graciously. Every eyewitness present at the Waffle House was lined up to testify and Janiya was eager to take the stand, Pawlowski was envious. "I don't get it. You have over a dozen witnesses prepared to testify and I can't maintain one." Pawlowski pouted sinking in one of Greene office chairs.

"I thought you had your witnesses?" Greene said back only in more of a statement.

"I did," Pawlowski said before retorting "and I don't! At least not one I'm confident in. My only witnesses are Xavier and Kimberly with Kimberly being the strongest witness however can't say I'm too confident in her now because she's thinking of recanting."

Greene eyes squinted, "Pawlowski you're fed, rarely are you guys this unorthodox."

"I know... I just don't get it. I'm here to finish what Selvester started, but every forward step seems like a push back."

"My condolences to your superior by the way, I didn't get a chance to say it when you were here last time."

Taking her mind off the case long enough to give Greene her smile. Pawlowski thought of Selvester and the mistake of telling him Marcey had had a child by Lil Ronnie. She would never forgive herself and constantly thought of her being the one sending Slevester to his death. Shaking away her thoughts she says "thank you I'm sure he'd appreciate it."

"You said Kimberly is thinking of recanting, you think Lil Ronnie got to her?" asked Greene.

"It's the only thing that makes sense" Pawlowski replied before uttering "I don't get this kid."

"Who?" Greene asked.

"Lil Ronnie. Here you are working on a case where his best friend practically threw his life away just so Lil Ronnie could continue his operation. He's facing life in prison and possibly more but can reduce that severely if he cooperated on the murders of Janiya mother and uncle but yet refuses. He's willing to spend the rest of his life in prison for Lil Ronnie and now so is Kimberly." Pawlowski explained disgustedly. Greene eyes had started squinting again, however Pawlowski didn't notice until she took a breath from all her rambling. "What is it?" Pawlowski asked.

"I was thinking about the name Xavier, he's one of your witnesses, correct?"

"Yes, but he is only as good as the Kimberly case."

"No that's not what I was getting at." Greene said. Than he went to her computer and started typing. "Last name White?" She asked.

"Yep, why has he been arrested?"

"Worse. According to dispatch, Xavier White was found dead at 6am this morning...is this him?" When the computer was turned, a sharp pain jolted through Pawlowski abdomen.

"Shit!" she exclaimed gasping soon as she saw one of Zay's latest mugshots. Pawlowski leaned in close enough to read the short article.

Some time this morning deputies of the Palm Beach County sheriff's department arrived to a dead body lying on the side of the road on Beeline highway. Identification found in the victim's front pants pocket identifies him to be a Boynton Beach resident, age 43 by the name of Xavier White. To anyone who may know this person or killer(s) please contact Crime Stoppers at...

"This is exactly what I'm talking about. We get a witness, and they die." Pawlowski expressed, defeatedly. She fell back against the chair hard trying her best to remain optimistic.

A huff came from the other side of the desk and when Pawlowski looked at Greene stare at the computer screen she heard "and unlike Mel this killer did not leave a trace of evidence behind."

$$$

Karen sat at the dining table hating the stress

showing over Lisa's face. The same stress that kept her up at night and drugged her throughout the day. The feeling for sure was an over the edge pusher and as the two women sat at the dining room table Karen knew she was committed to crossing the edge yet couldn't until someone other than her knew what her husband was up to.

Lisa looked off for a second after Karen had finished explaining Pawlowski visit and considered the mounts of trouble continuing to pile. A surge of hate was easy to form for the agent, however it was like she had explained to her son early before his teenage years. The police would do their job and it was their job to do a better job. Pulling on the robe she had slipped into before answering the door Lisa cleared throat. "Is there anything we can do to stop him?"

Karen shook her head instantly as if anticipating the question. "That thick headed man wouldn't allow me to see my grand baby because of his hate for Lil Ronnie. He'd die before being persuaded."

"Then why the hell are you telling me this?!" Lisa growled involuntarily.

Guilt attacked her soon as her frustrations erupted, and Lisa rushed to her feet apologizing. "I'm sorry Karen... It's just late. I'm stressed and my son is locked away and now sitting here talking to you shows how powerless I am."

"No, no, I understand all of it." Lisa heard Karen reply. "Every night I listen for that familiar noise that says my daughter is home and every night I'm faced with reality. She's never coming home because she's dead." Her words were starting to crack; nausea gripped Lisa through her emotions but before she could feel a real sickness she sat back down moving closer to Karen. Lisa hands reached out to hold Karen's and she continued listening. "Nineteen a young, educated mother and dead." Lisa heard her say. "My only daughter and all those nights laying with the grief beside my husband I feel like I'm alone. I can't even have sex with the man anymore."

A few seconds went by and as Lisa continued holding her hands, she noticed Karen eyes had gone into a distance gaze. It was like Lisa had turned into a bucket for Karen to let it out. She continued explaining how Lance actions behind things had turned her completely against him while occasionally mentioning not knowing where her own life was headed.

"To be perfectly honest I'm tired and need an escape....Lisa, do you have some wine in here?" She asked and the question caused Lisa to look toward her kitchen at the gift bottles she'd collected over the years. She had never touched them. Never touched anything after kicking her crack addiction but to each their own.

"Yes, their over there in the cabinet." She got up to bring a bottle and glass and as she did she heard Karen start back speaking.

"I know you don't drink anymore. India used to brag about how strong of a woman you were. Sometimes it made me jealous." She heard Karen giggle sincerely before adding "what was the experience like?"

When the wine and glass was on the table Lisa sat back down. "What experience are you referring to?" She asked.

"All of it." Karen said. "How did the drugs make you feel?"

Taking a deep breath Lisa looked at Karen unscathed face realizing the woman before her probably never had to face real problems. Searching for the correct words Lisa smirked. "At the time I thought it made me feel great. I felt nothing when I was a user except the high."

"Made you forget about all your problems?" She heard Karen ask.

"Completely.. At least until the high left."

"Ever think of relapsing?"

"No. Karen why are you asking all these questions?" Lisa asked but the street in her knew why. "It's not worth it, Karen." Lisa went on to say.

"Lance thinks I'm going against what's right. That I should hate Lil Ronnie because of what happened to our daughter but he's the one wrong.

Wrong about all of it."

Lisa listened but soon as Karen brought back up Lance all she could think of was her son being in jail. Lance had made himself a serious threat and although Lil Ronnie kept India parents out of his business she knew Lance partnering with Pawlowski was bad on top of bad. Especially if Lil Ronnie didn't know. "You know I'll have to tell my son bout your husband decision and Lil Ronnie will be mad about it."

"I know" Karen said sorrowfully "and whatever Lil Ronnie decides to do about it will not be my business."

"Are you sure?" Lisa asked.

"I'm tired, Lisa. Tired of the reminders, the hatred and mopping. Lance and I are done and when I walk out that door, I'm turning over a new life." Said Karen seriously.

Giving a look of understanding Lisa closed Lance out for a moment, focusing back on Karen alone. "Are you really, okay?" Lisa asked, watching as Karen drink the wine in gulps.

"Why do you ask?" Karen asked to drink more wine.

"Maybe because of the questions you've asked. I can't help but worry about you now, Karen."'

"I'm not going to lie to you. I plan to say fuck life and live it as numb as possible. My daughter is gone, my home is gone, and my life is gone."

"Don't want to do anything you'll regret." Lisa warned her.

Like a friend who refused the wiser one, Karen stood with a set mind. "I have to go now. Tell Lil Ronnie I'm sorry about all of this and I hope he comes home soon." Gesturing that she wanted to take the liquor with her, Lisa allowed it and watched Karen walk out the front door. When the door closed, Lisa felt sorry for the woman, but not as much as she wanted to because her nausea was starting to kick in more.

A spit of vomit came from her mouth just as she made it to the bathroom, and Lisa found herself dry heaving. Taking deep breaths until she had enough strength to stand, Lisa opened the cabinet drawer for her medication and swallowed two pills. As of late, her sickness seemed to worsen, but Lisa ignored it and kept it hidden. When she made it to bed, sleep was the farthest thing from her mind. Lance was the closet. Lisa knew that when she noted him as a threat, he'd signed his own death certificate. Rolling on her side, Lisa listened to Lonnie sleep and promised herself that, at the same time, Lance's death would come immediately.

$$$

The next day, Lisa was out of bed bright and early. Breakfast was made for the family, but she ate nothing. She couldn't. It was like her body suddenly started rejecting taste, and body aches were soaring to an enormous height, but she held on while at the dining table and pushed her way through. Lonnie was first to finish, followed by Ty'reek, who seemed busier as his age progressed. Left at the table were Ronnie Jr. and May, and both of them were staring right at her with their feet dangling under the table.

"What's wrong?" Lisa asked them.

"You were vomiting last night, Grandma; are you okay?" Asked Ra'Mya.

"Sure, Honey, just a little sickness," Lisa said, giving her granddaughter a smile. Neither of the kids knew she was battling HIV. They were too young, nevertheless, and their steady stare told her they sensed something. Were you spying on me?" She joked.

May laughed. "No, we heard Grandma Karen's voice, but Jr. wouldn't let me come down."

Glancing at Ronnie Jr., Lisa gave him a nod of support. "Well, I thank you; both she and I were having an adult conversation."

"Will Dad be okay?" Asked Ronnie Jr.

Through him, Lisa saw the complete form of his father. She had raised Lil Ronnie on life's truths. She found ways to answer each one of his questions correctly because she didn't believe in crippling anyone from manhood, and starting today she would do them all the same. "Right now we can only hope. There are a lot of people who want your father to stay gone."

"But he helps people!" Ra'Mya blurted.

"Who are these people?" Ronnie Jr. said right behind her.

Lisa saw their mugs and mugged with them. "People that don't mean a thing to this family. For some, it's their job, for others, it's just hate."

"The world has a lot of haters."

"When can we go see him?" Asked Ra'Mya.

"Lil Ronnie said no visits. That place is stressing him, and I know it." Lisa said. The last part hit home right there in her chest. A cough brought them out of silence, and Lisa saw the kids looking at her in worry again. "I'm fine. You two run up and get dressed. I'll find something for us to do today."

Ra'Mya took off like a rocket, and Lisa watched her along the way, thinking of Karen. Her thoughts had left the dining room completely for a second, and when she looked back around the room, she noticed Ronnie Jr. still sitting. Lisa looked at him, waiting for him to speak.

"Are you going somewhere? You're never dressed this early in the morning."

Lisa had to look down to remember she'd dressed before coming down. "Yeah, an errand for your father, but I'll be back in no time."

Ronnie Jr. sat there unsure and then said, "I'm

coming with you."

Protesting was at the tip of her tongue, and it stayed there. "Come on."

$$$

Red Tank, yo, y'all check me out!" Hot yelled from across the street, waving them to Lisa's car. Her and Ronnie Jr. watched them rush over from an abandoned house, with Red being the first to acknowledge her.

"Sup, Miss Lisa, how's the fam?" He said this as he and Tank stopped next to Hot at her window.

Arriving with little tolerance for conversation, Lisa gave him a light wave and then looked at Hot so that he could fill them in. "Fam ain't good, bruh, she's here asking if we're hungry. Watchu niggas think about that?" He asked, looking between his partners.

She saw Tank peer inside the window with concern at her and Ronnie Jr. Lisa looked him dead in the eyes, then back at all of them. "Whatever the price, I'll take care of it, but this has to be done." Lisa reported feeling a constant shiver of nausea travel through her body.

Last night, after deciding to take things into her own hands, Lisa thought hard on who Lil Ronnie would involve in this matter. Knowing they did all of his dirty work, she didn't hesitate in choose them. "Aight." Red agreed before asking, "Will this get our man out. Lil Ronnie is a solid nigga."

Nodding as she put her car in gear Lisa spoke over her sickness. "We'll see, but the sooner the better, so you guys handle this immediately."

Remembering she had brought a payment to motivate them, Lisa pulled a manila envelope from her purse, attempting to pass it through the window.

"Can't accept that, miss Lisa, Lil Ronnie will take care of us when he's out. You and the Lil man have nothing to be concerned about." Said Hot, looking between her and Ronnie Jr.

Thinking about them Lisa pulled off while feeling her blood pressure escalate. The pressure had made its way behind her eyes by the time she started taking it seriously. Making it as far as I-95 and Lake Worth Road, she heard a loud shout from Ronnie Jr. before everything went blank. Tires shrieked before a hard collision, and then everything went silent. Darkness came soon after, and Lisa couldn't hear, couldn't speak, and couldn't breathe. This lasted for some time, but eventually Ronnie Jr.'s voice was back in her ear. When Lisa's eyes fluttered open, lights were flashing all around them.

$$$

The food cart creaking up the hall made Lil Ronnie jump out of his rack, rushing to the door. He had been waiting for Spank to return to his work for days. Not speaking to anyone other than Tay and the runaround, he had yet to get the verdict on Zay. Lil Ronnie wanted Zay dead and was already plotting to send Hot over if Big Blue failed. He waited until the flap where the food tray would come through popped open, and then squatted at eye level. Putting his tray to the side after retrieving it, Lil Ronnie signaled for Spank to come closer.

"How's my day one?" Lil Ronnie asked Mel.

"Coolin as always. We're the only ones up there holding the city down, but we're good."

"Dats was up, Lil Ronnie said for small talk. After making sure the C.O. was not in ear shot, he asked, "I know your ear in the streets, what's the latest out there?"

"Bitch is live and in effect!" Spank boasted immediately. "Whole lotta shit big homie. Do you remember the ol' head, Zay?"

He heard Spank ask and perked up, but at the same time downplayed it by shaking his head. "Nawl," Lil Ronnie answered.

"He ran with Big Blue and the nigga Mel offed, but, fuck that Zay caught some mean ones to the chest and got left on the side of the road."

Shielding his smirk, Lil Ronnie straightened his expression and looked back through the flap.

70

"What else is popping?" He asked.

"Ya man, Derek is popping for real. Everyone on the east is screaming his name."

"Word?" Lil Ronnie was confused.

"Word." Spank chimed. "You set him off nice with that butta. From Delray to the park, he's live."

Spank words ran through Lil Ronnie's mind like poison. He was close to asking what exactly he meant by him setting Derek off nice since he had cut Derek off months before his arrest, however instead he said, That's what's good. The feds got me so detached from the streets it's hard for me to reach him."

"Don't even trip. I'm your ears, my nigga."

"Bet." Lil Ronnie said and stood, but before closing his flap, he asked. "Who is he out there with?"

"Couple Haitian from the shores. Think one of their names is Spazz or some shit like that."

When the flap slammed closed, Lil Ronnie began pacing. He had never heard of no Spazz. Never set Derek off with no work and never had an idea Derek was back hustling out of the park. His eyes rose to the concrete wall, envisioning the streets. He thought of how fast the streets hurt after Bell's demise. He remembered how the economy went down in weeks' time and pictured the city taking an even bigger fall now that he was away. Back and forth, he walked, listening to

Spank's words in his head. Where the fuck was Derek getting butta? Lil Ronnie questioned, and just as the question arose, so did a thought. His feet stopped their trekking, and for the numerous times since he'd been incarcerated, he wondered where Marcey was. Knowing the two knew each other, Lil Ronnie's eyes shot to a different location on the wall, ready to ram his fist through it.

"Bitch," Lil Ronnie fumed. His thoughts shifted, and like a slap in the face, Marcey threats of him being replaced ran clear. All this time, she had been supplying Derek, and it was all because he wouldn't listen. Putting it all together in record time, Lil Ronnie laid back in his bunk, seeing more blood than he'd ever seen before.

CHAPTER 6

Guns were carried one behind the other around the address Lisa had given while the three searched for an entrance. Being that the home was right on the outskirts of the hood, the layout was different. The sides of the home were half the size of an alleyway, with flush grass leading to the back. At the end of the house, the backyard had spread so far out that they could only hope nothing would pop out from the distance. Together, they all tried different windows, but it was Hot who found the entrance point, waving them over to the utility door excitedly. Telling Tank to hold up some light, Hot jimmied his pocket knife between the door, happy that the top bolt was not latched. The knife wiggled its way inside and under the bottom lock until a clicking sound brought the door open. Shushing them as he entered first, Hot led with a crouching crawl until pausing near the kitchen for view. The house was dark inside, with a little light seeping down the hall. Following the trail, Hot waved for Tank and Red to take the hall as he went in the opposite direction. He looked at the cheap appliances between the living room and kitchen, seeing nothing worth taking; however, as a diversion, he rushed through the drawers and cabinets before leaving all of them open and messy, then started on the living room. Before he could go deep into tossing things, he heard a scream that made him rush out of the living room and straight down the hall. Hot gun was aimed with his finger on the trigger by the time he got to the open door, and what he saw made him burst out laughing.

The guy, Lance, had jumped out of his sleep and pretty much painted himself against the wall. Tank was standing on the bed with Lance, jabbing the gun, knowing a bullet could go off at any minute. Red had also started laughing but stood back with his gun ready in case Lance tried anything. After the scene bore itself out, Hot told Tank to get off the bed, and without so much as a thought, his gun fired. Hitting Lance three times into the chest and once in the throat.

"Fuck the room up and let's go!" He barked, knowing exactly how to make a burglary look like things had turned bad.

$$$

Lil Ronnie III

The car wreck had turned into a scare more than anything. Lisa had blanked out several times, including what had initially caused her to run head first into a street post, but that was all. Nevertheless, bad news came shortly after the doctors read her medical file. The doctors told her the virus was starting to affect different parts of the body, but mainly her immune system. What Lisa had just experienced was a reaction to the stress that sent her body into overdrive and caused a shutdown. It was common to a lot of people, even those free of disease, which is why Lil Ronnie tried to keep her calm at all times.

Ronnie Jr. had left with his mother, fine and unharmed, and for a short time, Lisa sat inside the hospital room, thinking of what the doctors had told her. When a knock came on the door, Lisa told Lonnie to come in, but she hated the timing because since the doctors had left her, her face had become drenched with tears. Seeing them, Lonnie rushed to her side, cuddling her as close as the hospital bed allowed.

"Shhh, Lisa, I'm here, baby." He said, but no words can smooth out doctors revealing her life expectancy was nearing an end. Her body felt like a piece of lumber in Lonnie's arms. She wanted to scream, begging for the doctor's words to leave her head; however, they were embedded sturdier than cement. Her grandchildren would not see her alive much longer. She wouldn't see their kids, and more importantly, Lil Ronnie would be devastated. All of it brought her tears down harder, and she could not have thanked Lonnie more for interrupting "Remember when I was the one in bed and filled with depression." Lisa nodded and closed her eyes at the touch of Lonnie's forefinger wiping one of her cheeks. The contact made her pay more attention to him rather than the words floating around in her head. "You once told me crying would get us nowhere. That we have a child with kids, which means we still have kids." Lisa heard him say them and clearly remembered each time she had said them.

Her arm came up to pull Lonnie closer. Holding him tighter because what he said was true. Long ago, she remembered telling him the same words; now it was him, and she had to get over it. "I'm just not ready to go. It's too soon. Lil Ronnie is barely into his twenties. The kids haven't even started living yet." She babbled on. "What am I going to tell Lil Ronnie? He needs me, Lonnie, the kids need me."

"We all need you, and you're going to be here." Taking a second to remove her arm Lonnie was careful not to bother the IVs as he sat on the bed. "When I was back in that nut house, the people thought I was crazy. I thought I had gone crazy, and the only one who believed in me was you, Lisa. There's no telling where I would have been, but I know I wouldn't be looking half as good as this. I'm looking this way because of you. My strength is within you, so you've gotta find your strength as well."

The tensity Lisa saw in Lonnie's eyes made her head nod. She had plenty of sources of strength. He, her son, Ronnie Jr., Tyreek, and Ra'Mya were all valuable players of it. "You're right." Lisa finally mustard out loud. "Sitting here crying is making shit worse. Go get the damn doctor and take me home.

And just like that, the power had been restored in Lisa. She looked up at the ceiling after Lonnie left and prayed to her mother. "Get me through these troubled times" is all she kept saying.

$$$

Wilk Austin walked into his beachfront office as crisp as a million-dollar coin. He was still in his first ten years of meddling with the attorney field, but, ferocious in the courts and a born natural when it came to using his tongue or an ink pen. Ronnie Harrison's case had been given to him on a whim. A luck catcher with the case being as big as it was, but dealing with rich folks, he'd learned quickly to just do whatever they wanted. In this case, all he had to do was be the face while Blackman guided the work behind closed doors. A double header to him since he'd be receiving money and recognition. Wiping over his neat and trimmed goatee, Wilk sat his briefcase on the desk and stretched afterwards. His arms were fit enough to have belonged on someone's football field, but being one of the few brothers that lacked interest in all sports, Wilk's athleticism went as far as the page turning in a textbook. Vanilla creamed coffee came next, followed by the pull of his blinds to let the sun sweep over the office. After his morning ritual started moving him toward his workload, Wilk found himself booting his computer to read his daily planner. Often times, there's hardly anything to do because, just like Blackman, Wilk grabbed onto a slight number of cases and didn't pick up any others until they were completed. So what popped up on his planner seconds later was absolutely normal, that is, until he looked down at the bottom right of his screen seeing an email from the USDA department. Slate's name showed up as soon as he opened the file, and after reading Slate's request to speak with him, Wilk sat back with a smile. Upon hiring Blackman, he warned that the case may not make it near trial, and got-dammit! It seemed to be unfolding. Nevertheless, diligence came first, so before getting too excited, Wilk searched for lead Agent's contact number by dialing Pawlowski extension.

"Hello Pawlowski, this is Wilk Wilk Austin, lead

attorney for the Harrison indictment."

As a retort, Wilk heard a sharp sigh before hearing Pawlowski reply, "Yes, the young and vicious stud. What happened to Blackman what's he afraid of losing to a woman?"

Laughing with womanizing charm, Wilk thanked her for the compliment, however, his statement agreed to disagree. "No, no, not at all. I look at it as a blessing to the little league." He waited for a laugh in return, and after it came, he got to the reason for his call. "I was wondering if you could fill me in on what this is I'm getting into, he said easily.

Time lasped before he heard Pawlowski reply, "There's really not much to it. We have witnesses and piles of evidence."

Wilk looked at the phone as if Pawlowski had told a bad joke. Sensing he wouldn't get anywhere playing naive, he released a deep breath that was very audible to Pawlowski. "You know, with you guys being Feds and all, that's what I figured, at least at first."

"It sounds like your call is more than a briefing. What do you have, Mr. Austin?" Pawlowski asked forwardly.

"Not much." Wilk admitted. "Just a message from your boss asking to speak." Silence came over the phone long enough for Wilk to ask if she had heard him.

"Yes...Shit!" She fretted with a revealing

utterance. "Did he mention what it was he wanted specifically?"

"No more than I already told, but I think we both know what this means." Wilk said, thinking of the obvious lack of confidence in Slate.

"Son-of-A-bitch!" He heard Pawlowski mouthing before the call ended.

A smile crept onto Wilk's face once again, but before contacting Slate, he called Blackman, informing him of the news.

$$$

Moments after the call, Pawlowski tried contacting Slate herself. When he sent her to voicemail, she felt the need to pull every streak of her blond hair out. Rage fumed at her, knowing Slate was pointing toward moving behind her back and Kim's possible recant would definitely be the flat liner. Pissed Pawlowski picked her phone and purse up together and rode the elevator to the garage. By the time her heels were clacking against the pavement, she had the courts online, initiating a warrant for Kim's arrest.

Two hours later, she and several other agents were pounding on the Miami home, prepared to enact the arrest. The door opened, and the face Pawlowski saw made her face redden.

"Well, well, it seems you got the news."

Pawlowski heard a flutter from Marcey mouth. Pawlowski looked at the tall, curvaceous woman, feeling a panic attack coming along. Marcey seemed to put herself on the opposite of every end Pawlowski approached. First Sylvester, then his death, then Lil Ronnie now... Marcey, what the fuck are you doing here?!"

"Similar reasons as you, of course, the only thing is you're late again, said Marcey before Pawlowski saw her eyes move from her to her back up. "Agents, if you're here for an arrest, I advise you to contact your boss first."

"Move out of the way, ordered Pawlowski, " this has nothing to do with you, and her warrant has been finalized."

Marcey didn't budge. Inside Marcey's expensive coat was a smartphone. Pulling it out, she redialed Slate's number, getting an instant answer. The voice reminded Pawlowski of Slate ignoring her call, and now she knew why and why the message to Lil Ronnie's attorney. "There's about to be a big problem here. It seems some of your agents have been misguided, Marcey said into the phone, eyeing Pawlowski and the other agents.

"Is Pawlowski there?" Slate's voice said in a growl.

"Yes" Pawlowski intervened, nearly snatching the phone out of Marcey's hand. She walked off, listening and hating every word her boss spoke.

When the call was done, she had no choice but to follow orders. Turning to her men, Pawlowski relieved them but stayed back this time, asking Marcey to move so that she could enter.

Walking through the front door, Pawlowski saw Kimberly and Jackie both sitting at the table, listening to the chaos outside. Extricating herself from any tough guy role, Pawlowski walked to the table cautiously, producing her smile. "So you've made your decision?" She said to Kim.

"I did what was right, sorry," Kim replied apologetically.

"Selling drugs and killing is not right. Your protecting these people is saying it is okay for them to kill people like your baby father."

Seeing her turn her head powerlessly, Pawlowski looked to the mother. "Jackie, this is your daughter, do you know how long she's going away?" Pawlowksi said, pointing at Kim with emphasis. "For years, is that what you want for your daughter! You can stop this, Jackie."

Silence came from them both, leaving Pawlowski to turn to the only one left and hate the smirk on Marcey's lips. "And you think all of this is a game. Your family is not untouchable, and neither is Lil Ronnie. You came here and persuaded these people with money and fear, how dare you!"

The smirk eased into a thin line as Marcey six-inch pumps moved under her soundlessly. She stopped between Kim and Jackie, eyeing Pawlowski like a vicious shark. "You can say whatever the hell you want, but nothing in this room is changing."

"You're pathetic, said Pawlowksi.

"And according to my watch, you're going to be late to the meeting, or did your boss neglect to tell you that as well?"

Pawlowski's jaw clenched. During the call, Slate informed her of the meeting he had scheduled with Wilk Austin; however, her emotions were so wrapped up that she had forgotten all about the meeting. Backing out of the house, Pawlowski climbed back into her car and pulled away, thinking of her boss terminating Lil Ronnie's indictment.

$$$

After driving Kim to turn herself in Marcey mind went to her own dealings. Lil Ronnie would be set free sooner than everyone expected, and she was sure Lil Ronnie would be happy about it. However, while she was not going to tell him herself, Marcey knew only days separated him from his release and a war. She pulled up to the east side park, seeing the activity at full swing. Her heels stepped out and guided her across the street, where both Derek and Spazz were. Seeing her coming, she saw Spazz meet her halfway, greeting her with one of his kisses.

"We have a problem, Marcey said as he pulled his lips away. Looking at her, Spazz took hold of her hand and led her to the pavilion, where Derek stood. "Lil Ronnie will be getting out soon, and you two will have to go, she said, looking between them.

Irritation came as Spazz remembered their earlier conversation, but Marcey did not come to negotiate.

"Respects Marcey, but do you see what's going on here?" Derek asked her. They all looked around the park, seeing customer after customer getting served.

"Doesn't matter. I came out here to tell you myself since Spazz didn't."

"I ain't have to repeat that shit! Lil Ronnie, don't run anything out this muthafucka."

"Spazz, that's easy for you to say since you're not from here, Marcey corrected. "But Derek knows where this will end up."

Eyes turned to Derek, who in turn sucked his teeth. "I'm with my nigga Marcey Lil Ronnie, don't run shit and I hope that don't affect our business."

"So you're welcoming bloodshed?" Marcey asked him.

"What I'm saying is we're here now, doing business with you the same as he did." If he's not rational enough to see this city being big enough, then it is what it is Marcey's black hair took a lite breeze as she stood there. However, that breeze was not enough to cause the shivers she felt herself coming down with. Spazz's earlier words of choosing sides played into her mind, but Jackie was never the type to unveil them.

"Okay." She said, giving the park a last look before turning her back on them, "But it's your call, Derek." She warned, walking off.

$$$

The call came to Blackman soon after Wilk got it himself. A complete surprise to Blackman. Wilk's first call was to inform him that Slate was looking to speak with the defense team, but then a second call came from Slate, and this one was stamped with a time and date. The meeting was set for today, to be exact.

"Yes, I'm heading out of my office now; I'll just stop by on my way, said Blackman, who was in the process of heading to another meeting. "Why is Slate making it today? Didn't you just receive his emails?"

On the other line, you could hear Wilk walking through the wind himself. After his car door opened and closed, he said, "His first email seemed negotiable. It may be based on weak evidence, and after speaking with Pawlowski, I'm almost certain of it. But this one seems more urgent. Do you think there's a chance all this ends today?"

"If it's everything you say, it's very possible. Slate is an old dog. A real fed who hates anything lesser than a solid case," said Blackman, closing the door to his own car before pulling out of his office lot. "Whatever it is, we'll find out soon enough."

"Approximately how long will it take you to get there? I'll walk up with you."

"No rush, I'll see you upstairs; just don't let them start without me," informed Blackman.

He heard a laugh before the call ended, and Blackman thought of his clients. The Rouhani family was powerful. How much he had yet to discern, however, he sensed enough to know they carried some kind of persuasion in the recent changes. Reminding himself to never get on this group's bad side, he hit the highway and set his car on cruise control.

$$$

His car came to a stop ten minutes past the appointed time; however, there was no haste as he got out of the car and walked inside the building. The tardiness was a trick kept between defense attorneys and was the reason behind Wilk's laugh. They both knew no one, especially DA, waited for the loser, and by chance, they listened to Wilk wait for him victory would prove without telling.

Toting his briefcase with him for appearance, Blackman entered the office, hearing all chatter cease. His eyes lasered over the supposed bigwigs as if the meeting had disturbed his schedule deeply, but on the inside, Blackman was cheesing, seeing no papers out and the meeting had yet to begin.

"Blackman It's nice to finally have you here. Mr. Austin wouldn't start without you. "

Looking at Slate as he spoke, Blackman gave a lite nod and then made his way over to a seat next to Wilk. "Thanks" he whispered as he sat.

"The defense hates short notices. We're very busy, Mr. Slate."

"As I'm sure Blackman. I've been busy myself, dealing with this issue." Blackman heard something come from Slate as his eyes cut toward a quiet Pawlowski.

"Sorry to hear it, but now since I'm here, let's get down to it. What has our client done now, supposedly."

Three other government officials were present, and all of them looked over toward Blackman and Wilk like they were funny. "Your client has done nothing, which is why we're all here today, said Slate. Taking another glare at Pawlowski, he continued, It seems the people in charge of this case are after more of a personal vendetta. That in which I nor the government has any interest in."

"Sounds like you guys are admitting to a mistake." said Wilk.

There was a hiss from Pawlowski. A sound that came from her back upper and lower back teeth. Her first sound of the meeting, and although people turned their heads her way, neither of them spoke to her. "We're also here to correct our wrong, but first I need for the records to show that each party speak their claim to avoid a civil suit later."

Slate's offer was more of a pleading question. It was, however, for that very claim, but without even speaking on it, Blackman knew Lil Ronnie didn't care for any lawsuit. Freedom was their only concern, and pissing the government off would not grant them relief. "That sounds fair. Who's going first?" Blackman asked.

"Pawlowski" Slate called, waving his hand her way disgustedly.

Pushing her blond hair behind her ear, Pawlowski tried to appear as professional as possible. Nevertheless, her quietness and tight jaw pose told the real story. Clearing her throat, she said, "On the day of apprehension, our star witness gave distinct details involving her and a person by the street name of Lil Ronnie drug operation. Through further investigation, we learned Lil Ronnie real name as Ronnie Harrison, and along with his drug operation, there has been an extensive murder count that, up until today, is still mounting."

"Speculative" Blackman interjected.

"This isn't a courtroom, Blackman," Pawlowski said, back sharply.

"It comes natural now; can you stick with facts only. Thank you."

The hissing from her teeth again, but Pawlowski continued speaking. "I then forwarded the case to my boss, who then granted approval for arrest."

"For the record.. Is your witness still present. Alive, I mean?" Asked Wilk.

"Kimberly is very much alive and-"

"Gentlemen." Slate cut in "Let's not lose focus here. Your best defense for your client right now is to just get this meeting out of the way quietly, and I assure Lil Ronnie will not be disappointed. "

Tapping Wilk on the forearm, Blackman told him to relax, and they both sat back in their chairs.

"Wilk Austin, to answer your question, the witness is alive. She's now in custody and is held responsible for this mistake. Now to move forward as the district attorney for this region, I am surrendering Ronnie Harrison's indictment. Right here." Slate paused, lifting papers from his satchel. "Are there papers for both you and your client to sign."

"When will he be released?" Blackman asked.

"Soon as those are back into my hands," Slate informed.

Blackman looked at his stern look, knowing that although the words came out easily, letting a criminal go was not one of Slate likes. So were the other looks, but none were as sour as Pawlowski who stood, causing her chair to make noise. "You tell that murdering son of a bitch that I will be up his ass. He is going to wish he was dead!"

"Pawlowski!!" Slate shouted while jumping to his feet. "You have done enough to this case. You can excuse yourself."

The entire 130 pounds sticking to Pawlowski's bones zoomed past like lightening. The door slammed behind her, but Slate ignored it and stuck his hand out for a shake. "Please make it clear to your client that what has transpired here today does not happen often. However, this does not grant him a license. As Pawlowski stated, she will be up his ass, and I'm not going to hold her back. Got that?"

"So far I've heard my client is an upstanding citizen who's been wrongly accused." Replied Blackman.

"This type of arrest can assassinate a person's character." Chimed Wilk.

"How much does the government pay per-day for a wrongly accused inmate. Coupled with pain and suffering..." Blackman asked Slate.

"Pretty penny last time I checked." Wilk answered instead.

"Just tell him to watch his ass."

The room filed out with Slate's last words, and both Wilk and Blackman walked of together.

"You go to the jail and get Lil Ronnie to sign the papers. I'm going to inform his family. Take care, Wilk.

CHAPTER 7

Spank was at Lil Ronnie's cell door the minute word landed between the jail walls.

"Yo, Home front!" He hollered through the steel door. "Mel wanted to tell you to make sure you stay up out there and to not worry about him; he got this!"

"Stay up out where?!" Lil Ronnie shouted back, refusing to get out of his rack. "I'm boxed in like you niggas," he added.

For a while, no sound came from the other side of the door, almost making Lil Ronnie believe Spank had walked off, and to him, Spank's leaving was much needed. Stress was at an all-time high ever since concluding Marcey going outside of him to work with Derek. Inside his mind and throughout the night, he consistently wondered who contacted whom first. His guess landed on Derek since

Marcey wouldn't know where to start if she wanted to find him; nevertheless, fault settled between both of them.

"Nawl, this shit is over with for you, fam. Being in this dungeon can pull you from a lot of intel, but I do aight with it." Spank said, which only confused Lil Ronnie until he got out of his bunk and came to the door.

"What you're saying?" Lil Ronnie asked.

"Case closed, big homie, since last night you're a free man."

"Fuck outta here," Lil Ronnie retorted in disbelief.

"Facts big home. All the C.O.'s speaking your name."

The skin on Lil Ronnie's forehead creased as he took in what Spank was saying. He looked at the door as if he and Spank were face to face then said, Aight, I believe you. Tell Mel nothing changes, and I'll reach back to you as well as soon as I'm free, Spank."

Hearing Spank tap on the door as he exited, Lil Ronnie did not even think about laying back down. If he was getting out, shit was about to get heated because no nigga will be taking his spot. No nigga.

$$$

Back in the city, at the east side park, Derek was

getting tired of everyone asking if Lil Ronnie was getting out. Not even a day had gone by since Marcey had stopped by, yet the entire hood knew and felt it was their right to ask him. It wasn't, in fact, the question began to stir hate, enough of it that Derek had to get inside of his truck just to get away from the repetitive question. And that only lasted for so long.

"Is Spazz around you?" Derek heard as he answered his phone.

"No, I'm alone. Why?" He questioned Marcey. Sensing some bullshit coming.

"Why? Because you and Spazz are cut from different cloths. He can't judge what you can because he don't know what you know." Marcey said.

"You're right, he don't know. But there comes a time when you have to do what you have to do," Derek said back.

"And starting a war is what you have to do?" Marcey asked.

"Look" said Derek, taking a deep breath. "When Lil Ronnie had me on his team, he failed to realize what the fuck he had. I lost a lot of shit fucking with that nigga, and not once did I find myself playing cutthroat, but now the field is even, and my only concern is keeping your count correct."

"What if I paid you?" He heard Marcey say, and could hear desperation throughout her tone.

"Money isn't the problem. But to free your mind, I'll get with Spazz, and we'll come up with something."

"That will end up being the same outcome as when I was just in the park. Spazz is taking this as a game, but it's not. Derek, you know how Lil Ronnie is."

Thinking on it, Derek replied sincerely, "Let me speak with him, and I'll get back to you."

Putting his truck in drive and taking the thirty-minute drive out of the city, Derek pulled inside Delray Shores, ready to speak on Marcey's behalf, however Spazz was one step ahead of him.

"Don't tell me you left the nest because that nigga is getting out, he joked with one leg sticking out of his Benz. He heard the comment as he got out of his truck, and Derek waited until he made it to the car to check out the all-black attire Spazz was wearing. "Nawl, never that, but ya girl is stressing. "Willing to pay to keep the peace, Derek informed.

Getting out, Spazz gave him a dap-hug and then spat, "Fuck that. It's good money coming out of that park, plus she's only trying to protect Fool."

"Be it for his protection or not, we can't forget who calls the shots, plus I don't want her getting desperate. Fuck round and cut us off, ya'dig."

"Nigga, you think I'm clocking time with this bitch just to get cut off. We back out now, and we lose it all anyway!" Spazz said before wrapping his hair into a knot. His lanky body came out of the car and leaned next to where Derek stood.

"Delray is doing numbers." Derek tried reasoning. "Us leaving Boynton, put Marcey at ease, and she'll do whatever."

A breath of hot air came from Spazz's mouth. His arms crossed one over the other before stating "Fuck dat! The way I'm feeling, there ain't no room round here for Lil Ronnie, period! Just look at the shit, Derek. Boynton is your very own city, completely yours! What you think niggas down there won't choose you over Lil Ronnie. You're wrong. They gone choose opportunity, and you're there right now."

Derek didn't need to envision the image. He had gotten a healthy dose just by being the top dawg in the park for this short amount of time. The feeling was lovely, but knowing there would be bloodshed, Derek wasn't so quick to jump. "Nawl fam, that's a western movie ready to take place. We'll be dead or in jail before the shells stop, and I got kids." Derek informed while also thinking of Eyanna.

Spitting mucus from his mouth Spazz said, "Tell you what... You stick to the money and stay out of the way. I'll do what I do best and make this Lil Ronnie nigga disappear."

The words were dry on Spazz's tongue, and as Derek stood there, he tried picturing Spazz coming out victorious. Don't get it twisted; Derek wasn't lost in Spazz web of Marcey's. The dope game had always been his call, but now Marcey fucking Spazz has created its own war. The two had never discussed how deeply involved Spazz's feelings had gotten, and just when Derek was about to take it there, Beat-up and Brenda stepped out of the house, headed in their direction.

'Fuck it' Derek eventually said, adding that it was a win win situation for him, just as Spazz had said. All he would do is stick to the money!

CHAPTER 8

Fresh air hit Lil Ronnie's nostrils as soon as he walked past the county jail's double door exit. At the top of the catwalk, he stood there, unable to see the parking lot but overlooking the area as if he could. Before having the papers brought down for him to sign, saying that he fully believed Spank's words would have been a fabrication. No way - Lil Ronnie could not believe it until his eyes read every word of his release papers, and only at that moment did the things he needed to do rush at him for action.

Killing was at the forefront of his mind. Blood mixed into the night's air has his mind wrote Derek off as dead. Derek's partner Spazz would die as well, but Marcey...is where his mind drew blanks. She had done the most. Completely abandoned him while uplifting his now rival. The thought clutched onto Lil Ronnie so much that his hand unintentionally used the handrail for support. He considered Marcey not even loving him anymore. Moving passed him, and notions such as those only enhanced his thought to kill.

Dropping his head, Lil Ronnie knew whether his hurting her or not was out of his control, but one thing was for sure: he couldn't wait to see which side his emotions would take. "Mr. Harrison, is everything alright?" Asked Wilk, bringing him from a reverie and noticing the distress.

Looking over at the attorney, Lil Ronnie took in his tailored suit before gradually nodding his head. "Yeah, man, it's all just sudden. A lot of the things I was juggling mentally are in the middle of development. Leaving me with a lot to think bout."

Wilk looked back at the jail as if working out an idea. "You know there's a chance I can get them to put you back in there, I mean until you've sorted out the thoughts." Wilk joked, cracking a smile.

"Nawl" Lil Ronnie smiled back. "I got it from here. I do appreciate your diligent work, however. Thanks for getting me out."

"No sweat, brother, take care of yourself."

They shook hands, and Lil Ronnie watched Wilk stride over the catwalk; however, Lil Ronnie himself remained. His thoughts were still weighing on his limbs. Half a year ago, he left his family on an airplane, thinking it could be the last time he saw them as a free man. Tay was a mess. Lisa and Lonnie had to be just as stressed, and then there were his kids. Taking a deep breath, Lil Ronnie let go of the rail and started walking. No one was there to pick him up. The parking lot was deserted with the exception of a few cabs waiting for people like him. Choosing the nearest cab, Lil Ronnie gave the driver Lisa's address and then welcomed the stale cigarettes and cheap air freshener smell.

Cars, lights, and all of society were passing through the window so fast that Lil Ronnie pondered whether it was a reality. He thought of jail again. The small box of a cell they had him stuffed in. The greasy trays being shoved through the flaps. All of it made Lil Ronnie rest his head against the back seat, closing his eyes. Lyrics, books, movies, and every other kind of entertainment he failed to mention, he remembered real criminals vowing to never be caught again. That holding court in the streets was their only option, but not for him. Considering himself a realist and a realist stands on providence no matter where he is. A death certificate did his family no good. He got in the game to play the odds, so by playing them, he will continue.

Slipping into a light doze Lil Ronnie did not realize the cab had stopped until he felt the driver tap him. His eyes popped open and shot straight into his mother's yard. Her and his father's cars were in the drive, along with one of his. Lil Ronnie smiled excitedly, then strolled to the front door, running into an even more excited stampede.

"SURPRISE!!" Everyone screamed in unison, rushing him to the door. The first two leading the pack were Ra'Mya and Ty'reek. Lil Ronnie swooped them up and then fell into everyone else's embrace.

"Uhnnt uhn!" Lisa said anxiously, stepping back. "Put them down" she said adamantly. And when the kids were free of him, Lisa attacked and hugged him properly. Lonnie followed, then Ronnie Jr. Tay made him come to her, but kissed his lips so passionately that the company of everyone else almost slipped his mind. Being reminded by Ra'Mya and Ty'reek presence, Lil Ronnie behaved by pulling himself back.

"We're so happy you're home." His father smiled.

Lil Ronnie nodded. The feeling was mutual, and as he took it all in, his eyes scanned each one of his loved ones. Ra'Mya and Ronnie Jr. he noticed heights were sprouting. Ty'reek had not changed one bit. Nor did Lonnie. Lil Ronnie looked at his mother. She was still beautiful, almost exactly the way he'd left her, but there was something off. Lisa caught his eye, but an energetic Ty'reek did a massive take over.

"Grandma cooked for you. We got chicken, cornbread, and beer."

It's steak and Hawaiian rolls, and the beer is not

for you, Lisa corrected, causing everyone to laugh.

Lonnie led them to the table, and for a nice little while, they all ate with the entire family intact. The kids couldn't stop looking at their father, and Lil Ronnie couldn't stop looking at them as they were together, he was home, and the reality had finally settled. Lisa took the initiative and began filling Lil Ronnie in on the small things he'd missed, but then the doorbell rang, causing them all to grow questionable glares.

"I'll get it," said Lonnie, and he walked down the hall to answer it.

Lil Ronnie and Lisa made eye contact, sensing unwanted company, while both their ears walked Lonnie to the door. However, as soon as Lil Ronnie heard Marcey's voice, he bolted from the chair to the door. Before Lonnie could get a word out, Lil Ronnie had stepped between them, excusing his father.

"What the fuck do you want?" He whispered as low as he could.

Marcey's 5'11' height standing in the doorway did well at masking the insult. Her colorful eyes and perfectly touched face stared up at him and his anger. "I wanted to bring Eclipse over. He was asking about you."

Completely missing her not being alone, Lil Ronnie's eyes dropped to his son, and he straightened his face. Picking Eclipse up, he left

Marcey at the door and walked back to where everyone else was. Noise erupted once more with the surprise of Eclipse, but Lisa and Tay were more interested in Marcey being there. Both women looked at her drily before Lisa cleared her throat. "Hey Marcey, it's so nice of you to bring over my grandbaby."

"Yeah, he didn't want to miss his father's first day back." Lil Ronnie saw Marcey smile, and it made him shake his head. Fire was burning inside of him by her just sitting there like everything was cool. By just looking at her, you'd think she was sinless, but no one there thought it.

"Baby, you're okay?" Tay asked, drawing his hand to her lap.

Lil Ronnie blinked out of his thoughts and nodded his head. Then he tried focusing on the enjoyment of his kids.

"That's good to hear. Eclipse should always know who his family is and it's more than Lil Ronnie in this house. Marcey assured Lisa that familiarity with the family was not a problem and continued, but the dialogue with Lil Ronnie was like gasoline. Before making an outburst, he removed himself from the table and went upstairs to use the bathroom. Washing his hands after he was done, Lil Ronnie let the water run and stared at himself in the mirror. Right there on his mother's doorstep, he wanted to put an end to Marcey and probably would have if she had said the wrong thing. But not in front of his child. Needing to clear his head, Lil Ronnie dashed water onto his face and then reached for a towel. Using the toilet as a seat, he eased back with the towel over his face, trying to think. Marcey had "fuck" a knock came at the door, frustrating his perplexed thoughts more.

Without him having to say anything, the door opened, and Marcey let herself in, closing the door behind her. "Ronnie, what is your problem. Your only words to me were, What the fuck do I want, and what have I done to deserve that?"

The upstairs bathroom was not big. It was built for one person, and now with her, the space has become crowded. All Lil Ronnie had to do was reach, and she'd be under his grip, but instead he just dropped his head. "Don't come in here on that manipulating ass innocent shit. You know what the fuck you did."

"No, I don't. Maybe if you for once quit the tantrum and talk to me, we can get somewhere."

"Get where! How can you even come in here like you didn't just leave me for dead. What the fuck do you take me for, Marcey!" Lil Ronnie came to his feet before he realized His chest puffed with anger as his breathing attacked her.

"Lil Ronnie-"

"Don't Lil Ronnie me shit! It wasn't enough that you ended things between us, but to fuck round with Derek!"

Realization caused Marcey to grasp. Even through his madness, he could tell she didn't suspect him of knowing, as she tried rebounding. "What are you talking about?" Pathetically, Lil Ronnie laughed. "This isn't funny, Lil Ronnie. Who told you that?"

Lil Ronnie's head began shaking as he stepped away. "You know what, it doesn't even matter. You're going to sit here and deny the shit knowing it's the fucking truth, just get the hell out of here, Marcey."

At first, when he stepped away, his back was turned toward her. Quietness took over the room, and Lil Ronnie turned to see if she had left but found her crying. Something inside of him felt guilty. It had always been the effect of her tears, but he has grown to know Marcey, and if things were over between them, she would not be there crying. His mind started ticking. He turned until he had a clean line of thought, and then an even tone came after a deep breath. "Why are you trying to destroy me, Marcey?

"Ronnie, I'm not. I wouldn't do that, I swear." She cried, 'It happened by mistake. You know how I become when I'm emotional. I didn't mean for it to go this far."

"I'm sorry, but you crossed the line this time." He had stepped toward her, but only to leave the bathroom; however, Marcey grabbed onto his shirt.

"Do not leave me, Ronnie, do anything to me you want, but don't leave."

Lil Ronnie stopped. Her perfume wafted up his nose, trying to pull him in, but he fought against it. "Let me go, Marcey."

"No" she said defiantly. Marcey grabbed a side of his face and turned it toward her. "Please, Ronnie," he heard before her lips kissed his neck. Marcey then raised herself on her tippy toes and took over his mouth.

Her smooth tongue and soft body brought Lil Ronnie alive. The imprint inside his jeans was unavoidable, and he felt Marcey going under her own skirt, taking off her panties. "Not here." Lil Ronnie said, having to pull her off. "Go home, he added.

"Will you be there?" Marcey asked him.

Lil Ronnie looked at her breasts swell up and down and couldn't deny missing every inch of her. "I'll be there but give me time to wrap things up and be ready to talk." He told her, then escorted her out.

When he returned, everyone had settled in the den, including Eclipse and Ronnie Jr, who went to him first but shared his time with them equally.

$$$

Four hours later, perspiration was the only

thing covering Marcey's body. Her nipples still erect from Lil Ronnie sucking them. Her insides warmed and tingling by his pounding. The inner parts of her thighs still felt him there. Squeezing them. Smacking into them. But not before licking them. The mirror over their bed held Marcey's eyes. It was her time to figure out what the hell she was doing. She had begged Lil Ronnie not to leave her, knowing physically that she wasn't fully into it herself. Against her will Marcey found herself stuck between her and Lil Ronnie's chemistry as well as Spazz's sexy endowments. The latter name caused Marcey to recline in bed. Her nipples were now sticking straight into the mirror, only now her eyes were shut. Things between her and Spazz were supposed to change. The attraction should have evaporated the instant she went after Kim to save Lil Ronnie. Precognition told her she would want Lil Ronnie once he came home and Marcey had tried. She had told Spazz there was no more intimacy between them, but only seconds later, she and Spazz ended up fucking again. It was like he was a different version of Lil Ronnie and somehow did what he wanted with her. The worst of it is that Marcey didn't know how to feel other than having denial. He was out of control. A thunderstorm. But one that always made her cum; however, lying in bed, she knew sacrifices had to be made.

The water from the shower stopped Marcey

heard Lil Ronnie coming out of the bathroom and thought about their earlier conversation. At first, Marcey thought they would argue. That Lil Ronnie's anger would stir back up and maybe assault her, but she was wrong. He told her to explain herself, and throughout, he just listened. She went from the very first time she met Spazz and Derek, how, after persuasion, she and them had worked out a deal. His silence even got Marcey to share the details of her and Spazz's dating. If Lil Ronnie had any expression towards the story at all, it was then, and that was only a reluctant head nod.

After she finished, Lil Ronnie kissed her. And kissed her again. He kissed her until she was naked, stretched out in bed, and felt up by his tongue. Lil Ronnie sucked, nibbled, and licked her pussy like never before. And this was after their first round of sex.

"What are we doing to fix this?" Lil Ronnie asked, releasing the towel around his body to put on his briefs.

"Cutting him and Derek off is obvious, and I know that's what you want."

"But what?" Lil Ronnie asked, sensing she had more.

"It's the numbers. They've almost doubled anything we're used to. Soon as we cut them off, Tima will know."

Exhaling, Lil Ronnie collects his pants and sits

beside her to put them on. "Neither of them know you're going outside of me, do they?"

Marcey shook her head. "They believe you're making all of this happen in some kind of way."

"And once they're cut off, the decrease will cause complaints?"

"Or worse, Tima will discover someone other than you can move weight." As if air had been squeezed out of Lil Ronnie, Marcey saw his body sink in, and she sat up, cradling him with her arms. "I'm going to fix this, Ronnie, I promise."

"No" Marcey heard Lil Ronnie say back. He pulled her around his body, placing her on his lap. "We'll fix this."

"What do you have in mind?" Marcey asked.

"The only rational thing. Let them get a lil paper until I'm able to cover it all then we'll cut them off. But their leaving my city."

Marcey nodded. She had everything settled except for one last thing, and for this, she turned around and look Lil Ronnie in the eye. "Where do you and I stand?" She asked, but saw him become frustrated, knowing where it was headed. "Whatever you say it is, is what it will be Ronnie." She added, thinking of her and her uncle's past conversation.

"You know what I'm not giving up, and that has always been our downfall."

"Promise me no other woman will come along."

Marcey said after surrendering into her only option.

"There's only you and Tay. My eyes are closed with India and Kim gone."

Standing so that he could get up to dress, Marcey walked away satisfied. As far as she was concerned, Lil Ronnie had just solidified her decision. Following him out to leave, Lil Ronnie surprised her by stopping just before they got to the door. "For every reason you gave for me to walk away, you've given two for me to stay. I'll never forget you helping out with Kim."

A smile so big spread across Marcey's face, and the kiss Lil Ronnie left her with was barely felt. Solidified Marcey mouthed, closing the door.

$$$

The news of Lil Ronnie's release hit Derek late last night. From there, he called Spazz, and the following morning they both met up at the park far earlier than normal. The matching socks to Derek Kyrie 6 tennis shoes made a trail under the pavilion they stood beneath until stomping down on the park's bench. He took a seat on the picnic table, feeling the FN stuffed in his cargo pants pocket brush against his knee. In the other pocket was an extra clip, and as uncomfortable as it was for him, he knew it was necessary. Out in the street, his eyes flowed with every passing car. Even the people on bicycles were eye-scanned, especially those walking up. When it came time to serve, Derek would complete the sale but go right back to watching the road. For further precaution, he had Spazz inside the car about twenty yards away with the same level of alertness. Needless to say, Derek was ready and knew it had to stay that way if they were going through with Spazz plan.

For some reason, he expected one of Lil Ronnie's cars to come speeding up the street, braking to a screeching halt. Him getting out, raising hell before the area became filled with bullets. But after some time of no action, Derek began to question if Lil Ronnie even knew he was pumping out of the park. Or maybe I'm just panicking, and Lil Ronnie don't give a fuck! Thought Derek slightly before a call came in with him answering Spazz call.

"Fam, I thought you said this nigga would pull up fa'sure."

"I was just having the same thoughts. It's possible the nigga don't even know." Answered Derek.

"Aight, we'll give it another hour, then I have to go check on the wifey."

Putting his phone away, Derek checked the street again and sat back down. If Lil Ronnie knew Lil Ronnie would come, that much Derek was sure of.

$$$

In the Rouhani family din, there were three faces. One smile. One look of confusion and one plastering a beat red grimace. The smile belonged to Hazik, and he raised his champagne flute, cheering Lil Ronnie's liberation out loud. "What'd I tell ya!! Lil Ronnie is free and unblemished at last." His laughter carried around the room while Nageme produced an enervated smirk. Soon after, Nageme wiped the smirk away once he saw Tima getting ready to explode.

"Unblemished my ass! That cocksucker was indicted by the big pigs, only one thing gets you out of that!"

"Sorry, my brother, but that is not the case. Lil Ronnie's release is legitimate."

"Neither of us was there to witness this. The fuck is lucky we allowed Marcey to continue on with business, but that to changes." Tima Spat with spittle settling at the corners of his mouth.

His own hatred is the reason why he knew nothing of the mission Hazik had put Marcey on, if he had maybe he'd have a little more humility. Maybe. Rather than argue uselessly, Hazik pointed at the only other brother who knew. "His words are true, Tima. Lil Ronnie release was from the family's effort."

"So you knew Lil Ronnie was coming home?" Tima asked his younger brother.

"I stay away from the two of your disputes."

"That's bullshit!" Tima screamed, feeling like Nageme was switching sides for not telling him.

"We have been wrong about Lil Ronnie enough times for me to give him the benefit of the doubt. So yes, I did not say a word to you, and you're not going to make me feel bad."

Struggling to get up from his seat, Tima was on his way to storm past them before Hazik's hand stopped him. "Lil Ronnie's business will run as usual and give him as much as he wants." Feeling Tima shove his hand from his chest, Hazik let him pass but looked at Nageme. "What am I not aware of?" He asked.

"What do you mean? There has been nothing in secret." Nageme replied, unaware of what Hazik was asking.

"Before Lil Ronnie left for vacation, a package was left at Marcrey's. Lil Ronnie specifically said it wouldn't be touched until his return; however, the unfortunate happened. So what did Tima mean by continuing while Lil Ronnie was away?"

Nageme thought for a minute before saying. "Since Lil Ronnie requested to only deal with you or Marcey, we have had no direct contact, but Marcey has ordered three different orders since then."

"Are you sure?" Asked Hazik.

"Hold on, I'll grab the logbook."

As Hazik waited, he drank the rest of his champagne and tried to figure things out on his own. There should have been no drugs being pushed in Lil Ronnie's absence. Things become wrong that way. Counts are discombobulated or even short. He didn't like nor approve of it.

"Here you go, have a look for yourself," said Nageme, passing him the logbook.

As clear as day coded amounts and dates were provided for Marcey's name. Hazik saw what he'd needed but continued to view the log as he noticed a difference in each order. When he got to the third order, his eyes bulged at the enormous increase. "Has Marcey been taking care of Lil Ronnie's business herself. She knows we don't tolerate that."

"I doubt it. She blames it on a worker of his."

Nodding with a mental note installed, Hazik gave the book back and stood to leave. "Tell Marcey I would like to speak with her, and don't forget what I said about Lil Ronnie. "

"My word, brother, Lil Ronnie will be taken care of."

CHAPTER 9

"Spazz and Derek followed me to the house one afternoon. All of this started then."

"Who is Spazz?"

"He's a Haitian native from Delray. The one I've been dating."

"Have you grown feelings for him?"

"No. I'll never love anyone outside of you."

"How do we fix this?"

While everyone was upstairs asleep, Lil Ronnie sat downstairs in the living room, going over his and Marcey's conversation. He could feel her genuineness as she explained, but there were parts he questioned, such as her dealings with Spazz. She had lied about her feelings; he knew this because her words and the level of her tone were almost identical to the day she had to deny their relationship to her uncles. This is why Lil Ronnie decided to playthings so cool between them. Fighting her meant pushing her in Spazz's arms, and Lil Ronnie was smarter than that. He was also smart enough not to challenge the numbers Derek produced. Control what you can control until everything is under your control - is how Lil Ronnie saw it.

Feeling another presence behind him Lil Ronnie looked over his shoulder in time to see Tay's soft foot leaving the last step. He watched her walk over in silence and found her place on his lap. Her thick thighs scooted so that he could caress them, but Lil Ronnie did one better and cradled her.

"I thought I put you to sleep," Lil Ronnie joked, kissing the side of her neck.

"You did but..."

"But what?" Lil Ronnie asked his hands coming around to her breast. "You want more?"

When she didn't reply, Lil Ronnie switched their positions, placing her on her back. Her thighs came open, and Lil Ronnie loved the sight he saw. Glistening with a clipped landing strip and no panties Lil Ronnie made sure his mouth was the first thing she felt.

$$$

"Man, why are we still sticking to this schedule.

It's been a whole two days now. All this getting up in the morning is for nothing." Spazz complained over the phone.

Still having him in the car, Derek stuck to the same routine. The only differences were their clothing and Spazz parking directly across the park instead of down the street. It's better safe than sorry. I want to be on point when this nigga show" Derek informed before moving to his left, which caused him to step from the bench.

"Fuck waiting for him to show. I say we go looking for his ass."

"Nawl" said Derek. "Having you lose your cool puts me in the middle of a murder rap, and you know how I feel about that."

"What the fuck do you think is going to happen if he shows up here?"

"Nothing" stamped Derek, seeing no one where he thought there was movement. He started walking the park. "I need you here in case he takes things there, but besides that, you chill and follow along with your plan on your time."

"Yeah, aight." Spazz said in disagreement.

"What's your plan anyway?" Derek asked.

Hearing Spazz take a deep breath, he heard, 'First thing first, I've gotta make sure Marcey chooses right. Moving now jeopardizes that."

Confused, Derek stopped walking and looked at Spazz car from where he was. "So if you know that, why the fuck are you trying to blow the nigga top now."

"Because you're killing me with this scary shit, Fam."

Waving off Spazz's joke Derek started walking with his eyes on the street. "Maybe you haven't heard anything I said about those two. She killed her last dude for him, and Lil Ronnie loves her like the rest of his women love, like that don't wash off easy my nigga."

"Listen, I got my end. But what the fuck is going on with business. Since we've been out here, I have only seen like half the customers. What's up with that?" Derek had noticed the same, but with him only being able to focus on Lil Ronnie, he hadn't found time to address it. "Let me guess, because of Lil Ronnie, right?" Spazz adds sarcastically.

Without replying, Derek ended the call. Any street hustler knew when there were no dope boys out, money was jumping, and when one of the biggest came out, the streets made an impact. It's just how it was in the dope game; there was no divide and conquer. It was one way and if the dope boys were divided, so was the money, but it wasn't just that. He had to eliminate certain customers in order to keep order. Ones who didn't stay on that side couldn't be served. So deep in his thoughts, Derek hadn't realized he had walked out near the road with his back turned. A cop car caught him by surprise, and out of reflex, his hand shot to the FN, ready to use it. Derek eased his hand away as soon as he recognized the car, but luck was with him, and the officer did not pay him any attention. Feeling he was becoming too reckless, Derek waited for the patrol car to clear the street, then went and stashed his gun over by the lake.

$$$

"AhhhssssDaddy. Daddddiiiii" the sweet voice of Veronica called out as Big Blue sucked her pussy. The young thing had a taste of licorice. Spilling juice all over his face and beard. Every time she tried crawling from under his tongue, his thick arms would pin her back down, sucking her harder. This was Big Blue specialty, getting the pussy good and wet before turning it completely out. As a matter of fact, this was his third trip back to Zay's house since the murder, and not one of those times did his dick come out. Big Blue wanted to spoil the young tender first. Get her to the point of begging before giving her the dick, and she was seconds from being there.

"Uthh, don't stop" Big Blue peeked up, listening to her pant. Her red skin moved in waves, chasing her climax. Her body rolled in sync with his tongue, but it was only after Big Blue inserted his fingers that she started gushing. "Ahhhsss" he heard her say before pulling his head back to watch all of her nectar spill.

In only his boxers, Big Blue stood to his feet, letting her see the imprint of his boxers. Veronica looked down at it before looking up at him, giving him the go ahead but intentionally, Big Blue stalled.

"Is something wrong?" She asked when he didn't move.

Big Blue shook his head and took his time. Standing patiently before informing "I don't know if you're ready, lil ma. Fucking means you're mine, and I want all of you to be mine."

Rolling on her back with her legs open, Veronica swung them back and forth, fighting the throbbing her pussy was giving. Licking her lips she said back, "Zay isn't here anymore. I know you've been wanting this pussy so long as I'm taken care of it's yours."

The opening and close of her legs made Big Blue walk over, rolling her back on her stomach. Helping her arch her back the way he wanted, Big Blue stepped out of his boxers and then got behind her. Her small waist curved with a different kind of arch, and Big Blue grabbed one side along with the twenty-inch weave falling down her back. Wrapping it around his hand, he pushed his dick in.

"Uhmm" He heard her say, feeling his dick moving. Moments later, Veronica's hips were rocking with him. She thrust backwards, giving equal force, making Big Blue grit and fuck her harder. Sweat had started to shower his body by the time he rolled her back over on her back and brought her legs to his shoulders. Her pussy gripped him with amazement, Big Blue felt himself about to cum, but the phone inside his pants pocket started ringing. Big Blue looked over at the distraction, but neither he nor Veronica were having it.

"Don't stop Daddy, get this nut, babe." Veronica voice purred, putting Big Blue mind back on the mission. With everything in him, he started fucking her. His eyes locked on hers like a demon. Big Blue wasn't even breathing anymore. He was finally in the pussy and all it would take was a couple of dollars to keep her. In one final thrust, his loins burst, shooting cum all over her thighs and stomach.

Rolling from on top of her, Big Blue tried to catch his breath before moving again; however, he didn't have long to rest because his cellular started back up. This time, he got up and walked over to his jeans, which were thrown over a chair. One look at the screen, and a big smile rose across his face.

"Lil Ronnie" He said, surprised, What the fuck is going on, my boy, you're out?"

"Live in effect," responded Lil Ronnie. Where are you at? I'm trying to rap with you."

Looking over at Veronica, Big Blue pondered for a second, then shrugged. "You remember where Zay's crib is, right...I'm here now. Come through." The phone was pushed back in his pocket, and without asking, Big Blue told Veronica that company was on its way and to get dressed.

A thick cloud of smoke was in the air by the time the knock came, and he had Veronica answer and show Lil Ronnie to the back. Standing to give a proper embrace, Big Blue smiled as soon as Lil Ronnie bent the corner. They hugged and waited for Veronica to leave before saying any word.

"Nigga, what the fuck are you doing in your man's crib?" Lil Ronnie asked after the last of Veronica's ass disappear from their sights.

"Shit man, you don't see how tough she is." Pumping his hips in a doggy style motion, Big Blue made a funny expression, exposing his and her sex. "Nawl, but for real, Lil Homie, Zay fell off from what we stood on, so handling that for you was an honor, and this is the benefit." Big Blue spoke seriously. "How long have you been out now?" He then asked.

I've been here a few days now, and all I'm hearing is how shit changed. Niggas names are where they ain't supposed to be. What's up with that?"

Big Blue threw his hands up. "You left, and shit fell normal for me. I'm digging in old money now." Reclaiming his seat, Big Blue said, "I thought you were behind Derek. That ain't your work, he's pushing?"

Lil Ronnie's silence said enough. He looked around the room, seeing Zay's pictures still posted on the walls, and shook his head. "All that is about to fix itself, but what's up with this cat Spazz?"

Big Blue thought of Derek's sidekick and gave another shove: "A Haitian with a lil motion in him. Can't say much more than that." Seeing that look in Lil Ronnie's eyes, he asked, "You pulling up on em'?"

Shaking his head, Lil Ronnie said. "It's all cool, I came to shoot at ya hips some."

"Shoot," said Big Blue, knowing it was all business.

"In a day or so, I'll need you back in position."

"We're pushing the same way?"

"I'm hoping so if you can keep the rest of your men in line."

Big Blue nodded. Blake and Zay played things foul, but he was confident the rest of his men were ready to get money. "There is only one option for them. You push it and I'll handle them."

Standing to shake hands, Big Blue walked Lil Ronnie to the door and hugged the kid one more time. When he let Lil Ronnie go, Lil Ronnie left him with a small request.

"Throw Spazz's name in the air and see if you can get me an address."

Big Blue nodded before closing the door. When

he returned, finding Veronica in the kitchen, he walked over and started kissing her neck.

"You know the smell of chicken gets big poppa horny?"

"Really?" Veronica blushed before abandoning the food, dropping on her knees.

$$$

"So it's that time now?" Eyanna asked as soon as Derek walked into the house."

Setting his FN on the kitchen table Derek blew out hot air and sat down in a chair. "Lil Ronnie is out, if that's what you mean." He stated truthfully.

The utensil she was using to prepare dinner rattled as it landed in the pot and had her turn around. "So now there's danger to this house. Have you forgotten Lil Ronnie knows where you live?"

Derek thought about that. He thought about it the night Lil Ronnie came home, but making all these moves without first knowing if there was real beef seemed extreme. "We don't know anything yet, and I don't need you worrying about it. Lil Ronnie is not coming here."

"How can you possibly be so sure?" He heard Eyanna asked, but the question was one Derek didn't know himself. Like today, another full day went by without a sound from Lil Ronnie, and truthfully, it was starting to make him feel like Spazz really was right.

The entire situation was gaining too much focus from one side. He had already started walking around with guns, changing his schedule, and cutting off certain customers, all for maybe nothing. "Eyanna, relax alright." Derek said frustratedly. "Lil Ronnie is not about to come here. We'll see each other out in the streets, but that's as far as it will go," Derek assured, but he couldn't help thinking of the deceased Mike and his family.

"And what about you? You told me this would come to an end if it ever got this far."

"The decision is not mine alone, and the park is what makes our money."

"Enough money to cause enemies." Eyanna lashed pitifully.

Diverting from her eye contact, Derek reminded himself to be patient with her. "These streets. This game comes with enemies. You were the one encouraging me to go for it. Pushing me to my highest potential, well, this is the effect, Eyanna, but we're fine."

"We're not fine. The truth is all over your face. It's been there for the last three days. Stress and worry, look at you!" She said this, thrusting her hand toward the gun on the table. Eyanna added, "You didn't need this in Delray, just go back."

Rather than repeat himself, Derek dropped his head into his hands. Understanding her was not a problem. She wanted the best for him, and now the fear was starting to seep. If it were only him, this wouldn't even be a discussion; however, he wasn't alone and couldn't leave without Spazz.

The utensil was picked back up, and Eyanna left it alone. Derek looked at her cooking, but his mind was now far from the house. The thought of bringing it back up to Spazz occurred, but his intuition told him the only outcome of that would be a deviant reply. Shaking the frustration away, he told himself to stop. Tomorrow was back to normal operation, and if Lil Ronnie never showed up around there, that would be better.

"Yeah," Derek told himself. "That would be better."

CHAPTER 10

Once again the tenth park was in the low stages of capacity. It was the third time since him and Frank had got it up and running and like any other time Lil Ronnie wasn't worried. The few people out there were either unrecognizable or very low in position, however all of them seemed to recognize him as he got out of his jeep, sweeping his eyes over them to the many pavilions. Despite the few heads he counted the place looked desert. Souless, like the energy level had been depleted for some odd reason. The reason Lil Ronnie knew well. The castle charisma was down because the king was down, but not any more, he was back, and just as the thought appeared so did a familiar smile.

"Well I'll be damned!" tsst tsst tsst "Look what the white man the freed and the people done achieved!" Laughed Mr. Lane snatching Lil Ronnie in for a bear hug.

Lil Ronnie laughed with him. "It's good to see you too Mr Lane." He said, hugging Mr. Lane back. "The hell happened out here. I leave for a few months and you lose all hope?"

"Nawl" said Mr. Lane. Shifting the toothpick around in his while looking over the park. "Not everyone is out here for the money. Sometimes only the cause counts and when the source of that cause is gone so is the purpose." He explained lifting his arms sorrowfully.

Not liking that at all, Lil Ronnie took his eyes off the old man and pointed them at someone approaching. "Excuse me fellas." Said one of the men, Lil Ronnie saw hanging around the park. "A few of us wondering if things will ever get back going like it use to be."

"You know me?" Lil Ronnie asked, seeing that the man was addressing him directly.

The man nodded. "We all knew yous was gettin' out and some of the dealers too. Won't even let us buy on the other side anymore."

Lil Ronnie's eyes squinted. There were a few crack traps in the city so he wasn't about to go down a list of who's, instead Lil Ronnie glanced around while giving an honest answer. "Give us sometime I'll see what we can do." After the guy walked off Lil Ronnie asked "who is that?"

"That there started coming a little before you went in. He's alright never caused any trouble."

"There's a lot of new faces I see."

"Yep" Mr. Lane agreed. "I made the most of what you left me with. Put all the profits in the house minus what I had to use."

"How long have you been dry?" Lil Ronnie asked.

"Three months and I'm not complaining."

"Think you got the energy to get it back rolling?"

"For you?" Mr. Lane said enthused. "Dat ain't even a question son, we gone always be a team."

"Good. I'm going to set things straight in a couple days. How hard will it be for you to gather enough workers?"

Mr. Lane thought of the workers they already had on standby and replied "Not long once they hear you're back they'll drop whatever they're doing."

"Aight that's good to hear because you'll need them and I won't be here much."

"Why; you're about to go after Derek?"

"Derek went after me."

"So the beef between the two is real." The way Mr. Lane said it told Lil Ronnie he didn't approve. Mr. Lane's eyes barely reached him before looking away. "Son, I ain't ever understood street beef. Turf wars with people you knew all ya lives. One dead, the other in jail and for what? Money?"

"It's only business Mr. Lane."

"Yeah I know son, but damn I knew the both you kids all ya lives, you think I wanna see that?" Mr.

Lane shook his head at the image. "What are you gonna do, because Derek isn't the violent type."

"He gotta leave. That's all I'm asking."

"And it's murder if he don't?"

Lil Ronnie chose not to answer that. He respected Mr. Lane's honest opinion so pondering sides he would not do, however as far as he knew Mr. Lane was still apart of his camp. "What do you know about their movement?" He asked.

"Almost like this one with only lesser hands. Derek always sits far back near the canal and usually has the other kid with him."

"Spazz?" Asked Lil Ronnie.

"Yep, and I don't like him much."

"You've had run ins with him?"

"Few stale looks whenever I needed to buy something to keep the park flowing but nothing serious."

Lil Ronnie nodded while noting every little bit of information he received. When he thought of Derek sitting far back near the canal he knew only one pavilion sat back there and that pavilion was about ten steps away from a cemented trail.

"I got something you may not want to hear too. It hurt me when I realized who she was but she'd already started by the time she made it to me." Lil Ronnie looked over after hearing Mr. Lane's words and for some reason jumped straight to the wright loss of his mother. "She pulled up in that car a few weeks ago. Been there ever since. Being directed by Mr. Lane's finger Lil Ronnie looked a few cars down from his jeep and at first took in the unfamiliar car. The Mazda champagne color and clear windows rang no bells until Lil Ronnie saw a ribbon keychain hanging on the inside rear view mirror. Getting to his feet, he walked over to the car with Mr. Lane by his side and looked closer. The keychain was one that India used to hang on her mirror as well. Four of them were made. Two for her parents, one for herself and one for Lisa. Lil Ronnie opened the door to get a hold of the picture hanging off the keychain and stared at it. The car belonged to his mother in law and the realization left him both bewildered and infuriated.

"Where the fuck is she?" He asked, slamming the car door. He looked around at the faces in the park again then back to Mr. Lane.

"She ain't been here in a while. I was guessing maybe she ran out of gas but I'll put a look out for her."

Fighting the urge to kick his foot into the car Lil Ronnie stormed off. "Do that and soon as you see her hold her and call me."

The last thing Lil Ronnie heard was Mr. Lane promise before the door to his jeep closed out all noise. Guilt was the only thing that could make him feel dirty. Karen, a good mother and wife, driven in the streets for no other reason than the loss of her daughter. Lil Ronnie shook his head. He couldn't let her go out like that, not from shit he'd caused. He rode around long enough to seek an escape and at that moment realized it was time Derek got the message.

$$$

Carrying out his plan Derek arrived and got the park back jumping. He still refused certain customers and still had his gun stashed in the bushes but everything else was normal. Spazz, who was shifting in his seat beside him, had no reason to complain about their operations any more but like always he had found something to go against.

"Fam, this heat ain't bullshitting- its scorching out this muthafucka!" He said already half out of his T-shirt. Derek looked at him swapping sweat but paid it no mind. Florida heat was like a vitamin to his system. Like the radiation from the sun gave energy so as Spazz continued moving and wiping sweat Derek just chilled. "Fuck this I gotta grab something to drink. You need anything from the store?" He heard Spazz ask.

"I'm good. Just hurry back we can't get to laxed feel me." Derek told him before Spazz walked off and got in his car.

When Spazz pulled out something told Derek to leave the pavilion. The atmosphere had gotten too quiet. Following his mind Derek got up and thought about grabbing his gun but decided against it. He walked to the sidewalk where their lookouts and bike boys were and spent a little time there before going back under the pavilion. Not even two seconds later an awkward feeling hit home just before he heard dual pipes coming up the street. The engine was big but he could tell by the sound the driver wasn't heavy on the gas. Derek looked toward the sound and almost turned away from the approaching grill before recognizing the primed bodywork. He knew exactly who the car belonged to but didn't see any threat since the occupants and himself were cool. So instead of walking toward his gun Derek stayed by the road empty handedly.

"Derek, what's up my boy?" Hot said through the driver's window as the car stopped in front of him.

"Coolin" he replied but felt that awkwardness soaring the minute they started speaking.

"Shii'd let the streets tell it, you cooling it with more than just the home front. What's up with that?" Asked Tank.

Derek looked at the back window where Tank had an elbow sticking out and Derek sensed a gun being held inside. Not liking the pressure they were pushing, Derek dropped his nuts. "Sound like you niggas worried bout the wrong shit. Fuck y'all on Hot?" He asked the leader looking back at the driver's seat.

Instead of Hot replying, the passenger door opened and Red got out. The shape of a gun was shown through the window but Derek didn't stare long because Tank had opened his door as well. "D, the only reason you been getting money without tax is because we thought you were still rocking with our man."

"But that ain't the case." Tank said.

"Nawl nigga you been under the radar feeding outsiderd." said Red.

"So what you niggas pressing me bout some Ronnie shit. Nigga I been in these streets longer than him."

"You gotta get the fuck from round here." Hot said, cutting off the small talk.

Derek looked back at the driver's seat seeing Hot grill him. Knowing how they got down, Derek kept a tight face but inside he cursed Spazz for not taking his or Marcey's advice. They all stared at him and somewhere in that time the voice of Lil Ronnie appeared from nowhere.

"Is that gonna be a problem?" Lil Ronnie voice made Derek turn, finding Lil Ronnie behind him. Saying fuck everyone else Derek closed the distance between him and Lil Ronnie giving Hot and the others his back.

"Nigga, you really bout to pop off over this little ass park. You that envious?" He asked out of anger.

He was mad but aware enough to notice Lil Ronnie's hand stuffed in his coat pocket with a tight grip. Clenching his fist Derek stepped back. "I get it." He said. "You expected me to lay down after you shitted on me. Ignore how you repay niggas who lost love ones behind you. What the fuck is wrong with you, Lil Ronnie?"

As a reply Lil Ronnie's hand came from his pocket. His finger hugged the 40.cal trigger but held the gun threateningly at his side. "Negotiations were done while I was in jail. You didn't listen when Marcey told you to get the fuck outta here but you gone do that now."

Frowning Derek looked at the gun some more, shaking his head. "Do what you have to do man. I been here through these streets like every other nigga. If you came to take my life do it."

"You got until dark fall, and you can thank Marcey for that." Watching Lil Ronnie turn his back and leave through the canal path, Derek felt compelled. Stuck until laughter made him turn around.

"Do the right thing Derek, you know you ain't living like that." He heard Tank say before they pulled off.

The car door to Spazz's benz brought him out of his daze and Derek stared where the Chevy had just been. "What's up with that look Fam, was that him?" He heard Spazz ask, bringing him to look his way.

Before speaking Derek looked at the store bag filled with Heinekens then turned heading back in the park "bunch of arrogant talk but we good." He said visibly shoving it off but inside Derek was livid.

A few hours later Lil Ronnie's approach caught him off guard. Tank's words, Hot's words and Red words were all fucking with his thoughts. Eyanna voice didn't help either and it didn't help that the only one person pushing for the park was miles away buying beer out a fucking store. The beer top popped when he used his lighter to peel it open. It was his fourth. Far from drunk but enough consumption to bring out some rough edges he had buried. His FN was no longer stashed in the bushes. Derek had changed that the minute he walked back into the park. It was now laying on the table beside him cocked waiting on dark to fall "Man, look at this shit round here." He said out of the blue getting Spazz's attention. "We like petty as trap boys all over again! Standing in the hot ass air ducking police and shit, what the fuck are we doing?!"

"The fuck are you talking about?" Spazz asked right back thinking Derek was bugging. "All this shit is you. Every gram every watch out is the way you arranged it. Petty ass trap boys not seeing ten g's a day,Fam"

"Yeah but what seems to make sense really

doesn't. We can get popped to easy here."

"Fam, where is this shit coming from now? You've been acting strange since I left... Lil Ronnie?" Spazz added before running off with more words. "How many times I have to tell you that Nigga ain't shit. The few bodies he dropped didn't have a chance to shoot back or hunt his ass down. That nigga can't fuck with me Fam, I'll-"

"Bro, this ain't about no fucking Lil Ronnie. It's about our movement and whether that movement will last another day. Being here we're like sitting ducks and with him out, puts this city against us. Think about that shit man, we're at peace in the Shore's"

"We had an agreement, Fam." Said Spazz. But Derek could tell it was a point or pride thing for his partner and Marcey laid between both.

"Drama just never been me Bro, not for no money or a bitch."

"What do you mean a bitch? You know what's up with that." Spazz spat but Derek shook his head.

"I don't. You say the shit a business move but even when she came with a sweet deal you turned the shit down. Lil Ronnie brings you greed and greed is a steroid for destruction."

The Desert Eagle came from under Spazz's shirt and he held it loosely between his legs. "Call it what you want, Fam but I know opportunity and this the muthafucka gone take us there."

"We getting ten bricks a week how much more of an opportunity you want?" Derek questioned.

The question couldn't be answered and Derek knew why. This was about Spazz having Marcey. Not business and even if able to prove it what would he say to convince Spazz he was tripping; nothing. Looking up at the sky Derek saw it getting darker and stood from the table. He looked at his man wanting to thank and warn him. Thank him because he'd given Derek no reason to wait for Hot and them to arrive and shoot it out with them and warn him from the threat. Instead Derek did what made sense and said nothing of either. "Aight Bro, tonights a wrap for me. I gotta take Eyanna out and your crazy ass is about to fuck that up."

Giving each other a hug Derek stood back seeing his partner's diamond teeth glitter under the park's light. Out of guilt he hugged Spazz one last time in case he never saw him again then walked to his Tahoe. When the door closed Derek sat there for a minute and silently prayed for Spazz to leave the park early.

$$$

On the other side of town Lil Ronnie sat inside his jeep backed in the furthest parking spot from the road. The park was still in it's earlier state because he had not put out any work. That would come tomorrow, right after the east side park closed down. What had him back out there today was a call from Mr. Lane informing him he'd seen Karen. The news made him feel a little better but nothing can take away the pain after Mr. Lane told him Karen had reached the level of tricking. All he could think about was his mother and even in death the only person he thought to please was India. Those reasons alone had Lil Ronnie in the streets waiting while knowing the other side of town was about to fall to bullets.

Beside him on the passenger seat was the newest Dracko assault rifle tapped with a double sided clip for max rounds. He had brought it out with him in case things escalated once his hitters did their thing, but despite needing the release he hoped Derek left peacefully. That fate would be revealed soon but in the meantime Lil Ronnie's eyes darted toward some approaching headlights but quickly realized they belonged to Mr. Lane's car. When it stopped beside him Lil Ronnie got out and walked to the passenger side door.

"Get out." He told Karen after opening the door for her.

Knowing exactly who he was, Karen got out without resistance and kept her eyes low. The usual average size of her shape was luckily intact and Lil Ronnie was glad of it for the sake of his daughter.

"What the fuck am I hearing out here Karen, are you kidding yourself right now?"

"Ronnie, I just wanted to get away. I'm okay." He heard Karen say weakly but having been raised by Lisa he knew better.

"Fuck outta here with that. Smoking that shit isn't getting away, Karen. How could you even try yourself like this?"

"I'm not. I'm okay." Karen repeated shameful. Sympathy was getting ready to run over Lil Ronnie's head until the clearing of Mr. Lane's throat got his attention and he noticed the warning.

"Karen, just tell me why?" Lil Ronnie asked, taking a deep breath.

Despite her insides being filled with embarrassment, Karen looked up at him. When their eyes met Lil Ronnie saw a lot of hard mixed emotions, as well as a darkness sizzling past her sockets. "Ronnie, you tell me why. Why should I give a damn anymore when everything I loved is gone. India is..." Her voice trailed painfully before switching her words altogether "I signed my husbands life over because he was keeping up this madness and now that he's gone I just want to be free."

"Crack doesn't free you Karen, you know my struggle. Saw where I had to bring my mother from so why put this on Ra'Mya?"

The name of her granddaughter brought a gloss

to Karen's eyes. She fought the tears while searching for words to sooth her. "What does she know Ronnie?" Karen asked "That little girl doesn't know me. Lance made sure of that."

"That's not true. She needs you. I need you." Feeling his own self becoming emotional Lil Ronnie collected himself before continuing "It took me sometime after India's death but I realized there were still things here I had to stick around for. You are no different, your presence is needed Karen." Lil Ronnie looked at her hoping she understood what he was trying to say but knew he wasn't the greatest at expressing words. Not knowing what else to say he signaled for Mr. Lane's help.

"Is that who I think it is in the car?" Asked Mr. Lane, getting out pointing at the jeep.

Lil Ronnie looked toward his back door and so did Karen and like the sharp woman she was she started nodding feverishly. "No no no no no." Karen blurted ready to walk away until Lil Ronnie grabbed her.

"Karen, we all done been there." Said Mr. Lane "You feel like there's no love left so when Lil Ronnie asked me what should he say I said show you what loves you." A shriek exploding with Karen tears. She buried her head in Lil Ronnie's chest begging him not to let Ra'Mya see her this way.

"You don't love your granddaughter?" Lil Ronnie asked.

"Yes" cried Karen.

"Then what are we gonna do?"

Tears, wails all were heard or felt before Lil Ronnie got his answer. "I'll stop." Karen professed.

"When?" Lil Ronnie wanted to know. When his answer didn't come fast enough he asked again. This time louder. "When?!"

"Now Ronnie, I'll stop now." Hugging her Lil Ronnie told Mr. Lane to get her cleaned up and take her to Lisa's. When the car pulled off Lil Ronnie chuckled mirthfully then opened his back door to an empty seat.

Family would get you every time he laughed again before receiving a message on his phone that wiped all humor away.

In Motion the text read and Lil Ronnie got back in his car going home.

$$$

Four people were visible the first time the Chevy passed; however Hot predicted more after seeing Spazz's Benz parked along the road. Having no choice but to believe Derek had prepared for them they decided to go head first and yanked the car inside the park. The front wheels stopped on the grass with the high beams illuminated parts they couldn't see. Having the quickest eyes in the car

Red spotted Spazz trying to get himself together and jump out firing. Tank followed by letting the 7.62's tear through the bench Spazz had to dodge behind. Together they moved step by step letting off shots until reaching the bench only to find Spazz nowhere insight. Mad, Tank turned his gun up and started ripping at anyone. Red did damage to whatever he saw but his eyes were more open and luckily alert enough to move out of Spazz's way when a bullet came zipping from the bushes. In no time they returned bullets shaking the leaves with rounds but Spazz had moved again. Running toward the road while firing shots over his shoulder. Two people he ran between caught bullets meant for him as Red and Tank chased him but neither was a match for Spazz pace. By the time they made it to the road Spazz was skidding off in his car.

Hot pounded on the hood of the car to get their attention, satisfied at the work they'd done. As soon as they made it to their side of town a one word message was sent to Lil Ronnie.

Done!

CHAPTER 11

Courtroom 10b belonged to none other than the infamous Lucy L. Brown. Popular for the extensive amount of time she handed out during her short time as judge, most inmates considered her the blond devil. Judge Brown had built a reputation for herself where all cases deserving harsh punishment were sent directly to her. To the crime fearing side of society she was loved but as a defense attorney she was the worst kind of enemy. Finnerty hated her.

His eyes moved from the door tag that had her name engraved to the folder that held his notes. All of it was useless so to speak. Not one part of his notes showed doubt in Mel's guilt. Now with Brown as the judge he couldn't even slick talk the jury. They were fucked but he was professional and professionals always tried to find a way. In doing so Finnerty opened the folder and started scanning the juries they were there to select. In total there were forty-three names on the list. Finnerty looked where they all were gathered and estimated about thirty showing. Sticky tags attached to their shirts helped match names to persons and out of experience he tried to highlight those who looked to be in his favor.

Behind them were news reporters and so far the cast had not missed a court date. Three different TV crews total. Blake's parents were present sitting on the second row ready to enact the same rehearsed scene as every time. Mel would come through the door. Wails would erupt, the father would shout etc, thought Finnerty as he completed his sweep of the room. The only other people he failed to mention were the prosecution along with detective Greene dressed in a tacky suit that hid her definition well. Why didn't he look their way, because they didn't bother looking his. Not even so much as cut their eye his way and that told him a lot. They were roadkill ready. Open and shut case but all thoughts of his ceased when the detainees door opened and Mel was ushered out.

$$$

BREAKING NEWS

"Hello, I'm Stephanie Mills, live right here in

the city of Boynton Beach. We bring disturbing news. At some point late last night two gunmen were reportedly seen exiting a late model vehicle and opening fire on several occupants inside the park. The shooting took place just behind me, if you look closely you could see tapings and EMT fatality bags placed in various areas of the park. A total of two lost their lives and after speaking with several individuals here we have yet to locate a cause. If you have any information please contact us at 1-800-555-5555 to help reduce the violence in our neighborhood.

You heard it here first! Stay tuned as we'll continue to give you updates as the story develops."

The news hit Derek just as it did everyone. But instead of sitting round waiting for developments Derek clicked off the TV and stuffed his face with a pillow. He wasn't sure if he was ready to confront whatever today had to bring. Didn't even want to find out if his partner remained at the park. He told himself before going to bed last night that whatever took place he'd close the chapter on and deep down he hoped he'd be able to. Hoped one or both of them were dead and he could move on peacefully but seconds after he stuffed himself with the pillow his phone rang.

"Fam, get up! I got to holla at you." He heard, sitting up to the urgency of Spazz's voice.

"I'm up Bro, what's the lit reed?" Derek asked

nonchalantly before Spazz told him he was outside then hung up on him.

Derek walked out finding Spazz leaning on his car smoking the shit out of a Newport. "Yo Fam, niggas got at us last night." He said heatedly getting off the car while Derek approached.

"Saw the shit on the news when you called. I didn't know you were still there."

Grilling him Spazz spat "where the fuck else would I be. The shit happened soon as you left."

"Damn" Derek said in return.

"Fam, did them niggas tell you they were spinning a bin?"

"They popped some hot shit when I was there but niggas talk."

"Fuck, Fam!" Spazz shouted, throwing the cigarette down. "Them niggas could have killed me!"

"Spazz what the fuck did you think Bro, I told you but you not listening."

"I need to get that nigga's address, Fam." Spazz said pacing.

"Who?" Asked Derek.

"Lil Ronnie! That bitch ass nigga not bout to get away with this."

Derek shook his head becoming frustrated that Spazz still wasn't listening. "Leave that shit alone. The park is too hot to push out of anyway. We have no choice but to go back to the Shores."

"Man, fuck that, where does this nigga lay his head?" Spazz repeated.

"How the fuck do I know?" Derek retorted. "Lil Ronnie done been in so much shit he make sure niggas don't know where he lay." Seeing Spazz head back to his car Derek asked "where the fuck you going?"

"I know how to get this nigga. I'll catch you later."

Watching the Benz jet down the street Derek returned back to the house. After closing the door he saw Eyanna move away from the blinds and was about to question her eavesdropping until she hugged his body. "Thank you, babe."

$$$

Mr. Lane saw the approaching Benz far before Spazz got out slamming his car door. He knew where the car belonged and guessed quickly that Lil Ronnie had made his move; however instead of Mr. Lane removing himself, he stayed seated right under the pavilion.

"Which one of you know Lil Ronnie?" He heard Spazz ask, eyeing the five other people there with him. When no one said anything he saw Spazz shake his head selectively. "Aight we'll play that game." He said before pulling a freshly loaded Desert Eagle from his waist. Mr. Lane's eyes moved to the large gun while hearing the others gasp. "Is this what y'all want? Where the fuck is Lil Ronnie?!" He shouted, putting fear in all the others.

Mr. Lane looked round him knowing they all were aware of who Spazz was looking for. None of them had access to Lil Ronnie but for the ones who knew he did started cutting their eyes his way. "Son, you see what just happened at that other park. You'n wanna go and do something like that do you? Be smart and walk away" Mr Lane warned.

Mr. Lane saw Spazz's eyes turn his way before he started walking in his direction. "Always the one who speaks first ain't it nah' " Spazz said walking with the gun tapping against his thigh. "Tell me where he at ol'head and we all can get the fuck on bout our business." Hatred danced through Spazz's eyes as Mr. Lane looked at him but Mr. Lane would never let harm come Lil Ronnie's way.

"That name don't exist round here maybe you should-"

WACK! The gun cut across Mr Lane's mouth drawing a gush of blood. Mr. Lane let out a scream for the pain before cuffing his mouth all together.

"Don't fucking try me ol'head. You hear what the fuck I said!" Anger caused Spazz to raise his gun in a quick motion to shoot but one of the others saved Mr. Lane by attempting to run. "Take another muthafucking step!" Spazz threatened closing off the dude lane in a couple steps.

The guy threw his hands up for surrender but

that didn't stop Spazz from using his size 13 shoe to send a painful kick to his hip area. Watching the guy topple in pain Spazz's gun rose for the second time and swung the barrel looking for a target. "I know this is Lil Ronnie's shit and you muthafuckas gone tell me where I can find him or ima start shooting.

Hearing every word Mr. Lane closed his eyes in case the gun landed on him but reopened them when someone spoke out. "Lil Ronnie don't give out his contact info but he'll be bringing some work by here soon." The man speaking was known as Ted. An old worker from the beginning of time and although he hadn't given up all that he knew, Mr. Lane considered it too much.

"Whose he bringing the work to?" Mr. Lane heard Spazz ask Ted and Ted looked directly at him. "When?" Spazz questioned him.

Choosing to die before saying anything Mr. Lane dropped his head and again closed his eyes.

"Don't even worry about it. Just know I'll be close." He heard Spazz say before lifting his eyes to Spazz's departing steps.

The gash done to his mouth had Mr. Lane leaking badly. Using his shirt to soak some of the blood Mr. Lane cleaned himself enough to speak then looked at Ted. "Get the hell out of this park right now before Lil Ronnie find out what the fuck you just did." Mr. Lane saw Ted about to say something and screamed "GOOO!!"

$$$

For the second time that day Spazz sped down the street out of anger anticipating a run in with Lil Ronnie. No one had ever shot at him and stood round to brag about it and he wasn't about to let it start now. Throwing the pitch out there for them to tell Lil Ronnie Spazz knew it was only a matter of time. A matter of time before him or his gun men came to investigate what happened at the park and he wouldn't miss it. He circled the park after driving a few blocks and spotted the man he bust in the mouth jogging across the street. All kinds of ideas sprouted in his head as to why the ol head was leaving but he didn't care bout neither. Only that Lil Ronnie came out so he let Mr. Lane carry on and continued circling the park.

The gun was laid on his lap. Still spotted with Mr. Lane's blood but that was neither Spazz's concern. He gripped the gun and tried keeping an eye out for the G-wagon but somehow the jeep found him after he'd passed the wrong street. Wanting to be sure before jumping out Spazz peered in his rearview mirror using the daylight to see through the jeep windshield and slammed on his brakes. His hand reached the door handle but soon as he opened it a train of bullets riddled the door. Jumping out of the way Spazz threw his car in drive and tried to speed from more bullets but loud clinks constantly rained over the frame. The back window shattered just before he made another turn; however despite his predicament Spazz searched for a way to turn the tables. Almost a split second later he thought one had come when a car came from his right and tried to speed pass. Racing to beat them over the crossway Spazz floored it and tried to use the Benz's horsepower but a bumper to bumper nip caused him to spin out of control. When the vehicle stopped altogether he looked up just in time to see Lil Ronnie and Mr. Lane raising guns.

The windshield shattered first making him duck then more bullets shot directly into his car. Having no chance to shoot back Spazz did the next best thing and crawled under his dashboard waiting for the bullets to stop. It was his first taste of Lil Ronnie. The wrath Derek feared but the heat only turned Spazz on. Hearing tires speeding away he opened the passenger door and stalled in case more bullets came. When there was none he crawled out the rest of the way and out of coincidence his gaze landed right on the park. More people were out. The entire neighborhood seemed present but there was no sign of the G-wagon or the car that clipped him. To be sure he tried scanning the crowds faces and even thought to start shooting but before the thought could develop sirens started blaring from a distance.

Looking back at his damaged car he reluctantly got in and drove off. Catching a fair one from Lil Ronnie out in the streets wasn't going to be easy. Spazz needed help. A home address or something and he was tired of the pussyfooting. Taking things as life or death he snatched out his phone and dialed the one person he knew had the answer and no was not an option.

$$$

Behind the crowd Spazz was seen staring and Lil Ronnie was there looking right at him. Two feet beside him stood Mr. Lane. They watched Spazz drive off but inside both of them knew the individual was supposed to be dead. Lil Ronnie released a snide smirk, he knew there would be another time and promised himself Spazz death would be the result. When the Benz turned toward the highway Lil Ronnie looked at Mr. Lane's mouth feeling pained. "You gone need to stitch that up. Maybe go to the hospital or something."

Refusing to touch the swelled wound Mr. Lane brushed it off. "This ain't nothing but a sandlot stretch but, I sho'll wish we had got that muthafucka."

Feeling the same, Lil Ronnie nodded. He checked

his watch and thought about the business he had to get back to. "You good out here? Promised Ra'Mya I'll take her and her grandmothers out."

A smile tried to break out but Mr. Lane settled for a smirk. "Son, this life done got so normal to you you can kill and have brunch in the same hour."

Lil Ronnie laughed. "Something like that. I'll catch you later."

Hugging each other before separating Lil Ronnie toyed with what Mr. Lane said realizing it was the absolute truth. His heart was now cold to violence. Didn't feel it, and the only thing that kept him from believing he had become an animal was knowing his actions were pushed by protection; be it family or business Lil Ronnie would go all out for both.

$$$

Marcey had stayed completely out of touch with the streets. The past week had been nothing but love and forgiveness between her and Lil Ronnie coupled with them spending more time with their son. It was lovely and what helped even more was there were no more secrets. Not between them nor her family.

Pulling up and parking outside the mansion Marcey looked down at Eclipse and smiled. Today would be the very first day he saw his uncles. The first day of them seeing him. Family thought Marcey as she asked him if he was ready. The soft curls on top of his head gave her the cue as he nodded and opened his own door.

Hazik had the only heads up inside and Marcey found him waiting at the door with excitement dancing all over his face. Marcey hadn't even greeted him correctly before Hazik fell to one knee embracing his nephew. Squeezing herself into the mix Marcey introduced them anyway while laughing but peace only lasted so long. The minute she finished explaining who Hazik was, her phone rang and Marcey thought to ignore it. However time told her she'd have to speak to the person soon so she answered with the intention of making it short.

"Yes Spazz, how can I help you?" Marcey asked, receiving a shocking response.

"Yo, I need to know where that nigga live right the fuck Now!" She heard him shout and couldn't disguise her expression.

"Wait...What? Spazz has something happened?" She asked, trying to relax her face before Hazik noticed.

"He tried to kill me! Where the fuck does he live, Marcey?!" The tone of his voice screamed so loud it traveled beyond her speaker. Hazik looked up from Eclipse but played it off.

"Spazz, I don't know where Ronnie lives but you have to calm down. Where are you I'll come so we can talk." Marcey said walking away for distance. She felt an acceleration going on in her heart and knew it was out of fear for Lil Ronnie.

"I'm outside your place."

Marcey stopped. Everything at the moment was forgotten and anger rushed up her body and through her throat. "My place? Are you out of your fucking mind! Get the fuck away from there!!" She screamed but her thoughts were starting to flip by the seconds. "No I tell you what; stay the fuck there! I'm on my way!"

Her purse and keys were still with her so Marcey rushed out the door telling Hazik she'd be right back. Unbeknownst to her however, all of her uncles had come down after hearing her screaming. Pulling the newest addition to their family near him he told Tima and Nageme to go watch over Marcey.

$$$

The Navigator made it in time to see Marcey getting out of her car. Nageme got as close as a car length away then pulled over lowering their windows. A snub nose revolver was holstered on his hip and beside him Tima put his ear out the window while clutching on his machete's handle.

"Spazz, are you out of your fucking mind! You and Derek we're told never to show at my place again." Were the first batch of words the brothers heard.

Their eyes rotated from her to the guy Spazz, listening to them go back and forth. "I don't care bout non' of that Marcey, I told you what this nigga just did."

"What did you think would happen? You're still in his city and now you're at his home where his child sleep's. You're breaking all the rules, Spazz."

"Rules is out the window."

"No!" Snapped Marcey looking up just an inch away from him. "The only thing about being out the window is our business. Now leave my fucking yard before Derek finds out you've fucked everything up."

Signs of a man's frustration came whenever his eyes looked to the sky, losing patients. The brothers saw Spazz contemplating his move just before pushing his dreadlocks behind his head, and they were ready. Quietly popping their doors open they stepped out of the SUV but went no further. "Marcey, just tell me where the fuck he is aight."

"No Spazz! You need to leave now." They heard Marcey shout and although Spazz did not do as she asked the brothers kept to their distance.

"I'm not leaving until you tell me what I need to know."

"You're going to leave here or-"

"Say it! Threatened Spazz. He had no weapon in his hand but the tightening of his fist made Nageme shift until Tima waved him back. Tima looked over at him for explanation but Tima's focus was elsewhere. So far they were able to catch every word and every word was starting to bring Tima interest. "Call him here, Marcey!"

"I don't need Lil Ronnie for you. I'll kill you my fucking-" before the last word could come out Spazz had reacted and yoked her by the neck. In one motion he slung her body against the car jacking her up.

"You won't kill a fucking thing. You belong to me, Marcey."

"Let her go! Get your fucking hands off her right now." The shouting voice of Nageme caused Spazz and Marcey both to look. Spazz however had to look over his shoulder and only saw Nageme pointing a gun at him and thought to use Marcey as a shield and go for his gun but fat or not Tima was one step ahead of him.

"You reach for that gun I'll chop your fucking head off. Tims said, making Spazz look back toward the car seeing Tima standing on the hood. For some reason the machete looked more threatening than the gun and knew if he tried anything one or the other would beat him to the punch. Feeling Nageme come and snatch the gun from his waist Spazz let Marcey go and ended up eating a vicious slap from her as soon as he did.

"I should kill you right now!" Marcey shouted.

Getting so riled up she wanted to slap him again.

Climbing from the car Tima told Marcey to back off and looked Spazz over. "What is your problem?" Tima asked, his accent interfering with his words a little.

"Yo y'all can do whatever the fuck you want to me but that nigga's dead." Spazz said not giving a fuck who they were.

"Whose dead?" Tima asked

"Shut up! Spazz, don't you say a fucking word." Interrupted Marcey wanting her uncles out of her business.

"Lil Ronnie" Spazz said anyway.

When Marcey went to curse him for it Tima screamed for her to be quiet. He then turned and looked at Spazz. "So you and Lil Ronnie have beef but you are at my niece place with your hand around her fucking neck." Tima said his voice starting to simmer with anger.

"She knows why I'm here."

"But I don't. Who are you?" Tima questioned.

"He was a friend of mine but that is no more." Stated Marcey. Her eyes warned Spazz to keep his mouth shut.

The word slut was at the tip of Tima tongue but Tima held it for later and stayed on Spazz. "Is there any more to it than you fucking her?"

"We do business together."

Derek and I do business. You are nothing and

Derek will know." Corrected Marcey.

The machete in Tima's hand turned into a cane as he rested on it. Things with Marcey as of late were now starting to unravel but Tima realized they had it all wrong "so you don't work for Lil Ronnie?"

Spazz shook his head. "Fuck no. We do our own thing and now this nigga is out she's letting him step on that."

"You're a liar you're mad because of me!" Marcey shouted. Angered by what Spazz was saying.

"But have you been giving him our dope?" Tima asked.

"No not him."

'And not Lil Ronnie then who?" Seeing his question brought silence Tima did the math on his own. "Derek?"

"None of that has to do with this why are y'all here?" Marcey asked, looking at him and Nageme.

"Hazik thought-"

"Hush Nageme, we don't owe an explanation." Tima looked back at Spazz "has your partner been pushing our product?"

"Quicker than he can get it. Marcey knows this but it ain't about the money for her."

"And it's not about the money for you either." Marcey shouted right back.

Tima, tired of telling Marcey to be quiet, didn't even bother. He had discovered more than he'd expected. Who would have known. He thought while asking "where can I find Derek?"

"Tima, you don't want to do this." Marcey said, knowing where he was about to take things. "You're not the leader. Nageme do something." She panicked.

"Where can I find him?" He repeated to Spazz, ignoring Marcey.

Understanding what was going on Spazz nodded for his gun and Tima consented. "I'll take you to him but I didn't come here for business." Spazz said, sticking his gun in his pants.

"Two birds my friend... Two birds one stone."

With those words Spazz joined Tima and Marcey was left with Nageme. She stared at her uncle disappointedly, "He's out of control, Nageme you should have done something!"

CHAPTER 12

Pawlowski felt as if there was a load of feces attached to her body the way she went about her days. Her office, on the way to it or anything concerning law enforcement sickened her nerve system. Slate's voice often disturbed her sleep whenever she could sleep. And it wasn't just about him letting Lil Ronnie go. No, the worse came after. Him telling their coworkers and them believing she was a fuck up. The grimace he gave during their passings, and the meetings she had to attend were almost unbearable. Further Pawlowski had not received a single case since. The pitbull in her was now a poodle and she was lucky for that however her intelligence was also fading.

"Oh get a grip Pawlowski, I'm sure it's not as bad as you're making it to be." Informed Greene tired of Pawlowski complaining after just a minute of her arrival.

"It is. I've actually considered applying here." Pawlowski replied suggestively but weakly. "No one there never liked me from the beginning." She pouted more.

"That statement is your emotions and you'd actually give up that big office of yours to work in this dump?"

Looking around Greene's office, Pawlowski quickly recanted the thought. She'd forgotten just how cramped and muddy it was. "Maybe I am over reacting a little. I just..." Her voice trailed to take a breath. "Hate being an outsider. Hate being blamed."

"Imagine how I feel arresting blacks and hearing my own kind call me a trader. We're the bad guys and when we don't get the bad guy we're still the bad guys."

"I seriously can't go on like this." Pawlowski professed her body sinking into the chair.

"Then what are you planning to do about it?" Greene asked.

"I have no idea"

"Well I can tell you where to start." Said Greene looking over the wrinkled jeans and shirt she had on. Her hair was not its best either, after a minute of catching Greene stare, Pawlowski's face squinted.

"Are you implying-"

"A shower, yes. You're not sleeping either." Greene sat up in her chair pitifully looking at her. Pawlowski, you're going through your shit and I understand but it's probably why you haven't received another case yet."

Throwing away any look of defense, Pawlowski considered Greene's advice. "Maybe you're right." She agreed. "But then I'll be home rested and still wondering what to do with my life."

"Or you could use the time to break down and rebuild the case with unbiasedness."

"But the case was handled correctly." Pawlowski protested.

"Probably but let's face it. Selvester let you in on a very unorthodox case. A case you probably would have done better on if it wasn't handed down from a lover." Sitting back in her seat Greene added "Just try and see what you come up with."

"I like that." Admitted Pawlowski. "I should really go back at Lil Ronnie. Lil Ronnie and Marcey."

"No Pawlowski" Greene shook her head seeing she had it wrong. "You should work the weak ends and come up with whatever you come up with."

Calming herself Pawlowski thought long on it then stood and collected her bags. "Thank you detective I'm glad I stopped by."

Nodding out her welcome Greene asked her one final question "Where are you heading now?"

Pawlowski flushed a smile as she said "Shower

as you suggested, then I'm getting laid. Sex always helps me think." Pawlowski informed. Spinning on her heels and heading out the door.

$$$

The sequence of events had Derek's head spinning. Spazz had gone from having the park shot up, to getting shot at, not once but twice, to getting a plug all in a twenty-four hour span. The chain of events flipped through Derek's head so fast Spazz and Tima were almost a blur standing in front of him. How this happened he had no clue but he continued listening as the conversation switched from Spazz to the offer Tima came with. As Tima talked Derek tried seeing a resemblance between Marcey and him but there wasn't much outside his foreign look. Truthfully Derek was hoping they were some kin because things he were saying could really lift them.

"I can't lie, it don't seem real. Most people who create a disruption get the complete opposite of what you're offering. This gotta be the wildest shit I ever heard." Derek informed after hearing Tima's pitch.

He saw Tima nod. His hands moving inside his pockets as they stood in his living room. Without asking, Derek saw Tima walk over to one of his couches taking himself a seat. "Lil Ronnie has never been my choice." Tima told him once seated. "Meeting Spazz helped solidify things I've already had in works. This is an opportunity and one you shouldn't have to second guess."

"I just like things to make sense." Derek said straight up.

"As do I. I can always go elsewhere if you need time to think." He heard Tima say.

Derek looked at him. Something about Tima told him the man wasn't the man. That what was transpiring was a rush. A desperate move but despite Tima's will to make him uncomfortable he couldn't deny Tima allure of being connected and at the moment that's what mattered. "Nawl all is good." Derek said, glancing at Spazz. "So to get this straight you're gonna start dealing with us and all we have to do is move the work?"

"No" Tima said. Sitting up to make himself very clear. "I'm dealing with you directly. Spazz will have a different agenda."

Knowing that had to be related to killing Lil Ronnie, Derek spoke to make things clear. "I'm not interested in staying in this city so you don't have to go after Lil Ronnie for it."

Spazz's feet shifted ready to fight his decision but then Derek saw Tima signal him to silence and knew they'd spoken of their deal beforehand. "An enemy is an enemy and ones like Lil Ronnie can't be left walking, Derek." Tima said producing a smirk.

"I don't have enemies." Derek told him seriously.

"But Spazz do and Spazz is apart of your team correct?"

Derek looked over at Spazz who could be seen mugging him to comply, however Derek was a man who stood on certain beliefs. "He makes the team but-"

"No, no leave the butts to women now." Tima joked, his finger wagging back and forth to conclude the topic. When he saw Derek ready to listen he asked "how much can you handle and we'll see things off as soon as possible."

"For now we'll stick with what we've been getting. Things will take a step back before moving forward but you won't notice. The numbers will double again in no time."

"Fine." Tima agreed standing "but there's one thing I must ask." He added.

"What's that?" Derek replied.

"All ties are cut off from anyone of my family. For now on, you work with me. You answer to me only understood."

Derek nodded. That was one thing he agreed with completely.

He walked them to the door and saw them out; however, he went as far as his threshold. Only after they made it to the car did he shut the house door but ended up watching from the window. That feeling about Tima stayed with Derek. Somewhere a mistake was being made and he couldn't pinpoint it. Like now, as they stopped outside the car to talk there weren't any pleasant smiles from a completed business arraignment. Only hard stares and head nods. Definitely not what Derek expected but again for a direct connection he'd find his own way to become comfortable.

$$$

Marcey felt the need to inform Lil Ronnie. Let him know things had slipped from her hands. That she was no longer in control. But how the hell could she without getting him mad. The thought alone of him leaving her made Marcey shake her head. "No" She told herself pacing inside her home. "You got this! Just take care of it and Lil Ronnie will never know." But as she said it her fight with Spazz came to mind making her curse. "Dammit" she hissed remembering all of the fuck yous she'd sent his way knowing he would have been her easiest asset.

Never breaking her pacing Marcey bit down on her knuckles and tried to think of another way. She thought of her uncle and wanted to draw blood for Tima's actions. He'd really done it this time but she couldn't just sit there and throw fits. She had to start making calls and the only other person she could think of was probably mad at her as well.

"Hello Derek, have you seen or heard from Spazz?" She asked soon as Derek answered his phone.

"Nawl. Haven't seen anyone." She heard him reply and did not miss his dryness.

He was lying' Marcey mind screamed but now wasn't the time for bullshit. "Derek, don't fuck with me right now okay. I know Spazz met with you. Him and my uncle, what are they planning?"

"Aye, what the fuck ya'll got going on?" She heard him ask as if he was the one upset.

"Derek, just tell me alright."

There was a mumble of some sort at first but then she heard "Spazz and I spoke but I'm out of the beef shit and you can let Lil Ronnie know that."

That was all she got before the phone clicked in her ear. Jackie thought of calling back. She needed more info. Too much was missing. Like she knew he'd met with Tima but he did not mention it. However she put the phone down and tried connecting the few dots she already had. Tima was interested in Derek and if they met Derek was given a deal. Tima also wanted Lil Ronnie out of the way and with Spazz now being with him the desire had quadrupled. Is that what Derek meant by being out of it? It was possible since he likes to avoid bloodshed. She thought but couldn't say for sure. Marcey walked in her room and sat on the bed. The blankets from when her and Lil Ronnie had sex was still there and she reached her hand out as if it was his body. She felt thinking that she could lose him. Not now she told herself. Not ever, she was willing to do whatever to keep him safe. Thinking through the remainder of her options Marcey thought of begging her uncle. Asking him to call off whatever he had in mind but knew that would be a waste. He hadn't respected her since the death of Bell and that is probably how their relationship would end. Then she thought of Spazz. He was wild and crazy and pressed to kill Lil Ronnie but had an unquenching thirst for her... Had an unquenching thirst for her!! The thought jumped out at her and Marcey stood up from the bed. She searched for where she'd put her phone and dialed his number.

"It's gonna work...pick up, pick up, pick up." She chanted as his phone began ringing.

$$$

Sitting as comfortable as she could on one of the county jail visiting stools, Ja'nell noticed Mel more distant than usual. They talked but there was no humor nor laughter and she couldn't help but wonder if the recent events were getting to him. A pause came between them and being the concerned person she was she tapped on the plexiglass that separated them getting his attention.

"Are you okay?" She asked, throwing loose

braids of hair over her back.

"Yeah, all is good just ready to get over the end of this shit." He said, barely moving his blackened lips.

"Is it getting to you?" She asked.

"Nawl I still don't regret anything. My man was getting miss handled and sometimes this is the outcome to fixing it." His right palm opened and Mel was seen glancing at it for a moment. Almost like contemplating on something but before she could ask he started back speaking. "If there's anything I hate about this shit it's Janiya. She doesn't deserve this." His palm closed into a fist and his arm extended as if stretching. "It's always been fucked up for her."

Ja'nell was far from cold hearted or maybe she just loved and wanted Mel home too much but the sympathy she saw coming over his face was not mutual. "She's testifying."

"And I don't blame her. Can you imagine seeing your mother shot the fuck up at that age?" Mel said. "Then I give her my word and not even an hour later she see me doing the same shit she just accused me of." Shaking his head he had to look away for ja'nell not to see his anger. "What happened out there with your pop's?"

The topic was switched so fast Ja'nell just went with it. Looking over both her shoulders before speaking, she said "a guy came by looking for Lil

Ronnie and no one would speak he chose my father to send a message through."

"Might be the same nigga with Derek." She heard Mel say in thought and for clarification she added.

"Tall with dreads?"

"Yeah, that sounds like the one I'm hearing bout. Did your father respond?" Mel asked for retaliation.

"Yep" Ja'nell bragged about being present at the time of the shooting. "The guy kept circling the area until he was blocked off and..."

"I get it." Mel said, hearing enough. "Sorry to hear that shit came at your pop's."

Ja'nell nodded but for a different reason. "Thanks but at this point I'm not even sorry for him. My father has been one of the strongest men I know. Very wise and could have taken what he'd earned from Lil Ronnie and went legitimate a long time ago. But he's no different then you when it comes to Lil Ronnie."

Truth of the statement made Mel stare at her, more than not looking to see if she approved. However, Ja'nell's feelings were in between. She knew what the streets did and was experiencing the consequences firsthand and if she knew, she guessed they had to know. "Ja'nell, we both know how this is going to end for me. I chose my decisions and I won't fault you for choosing yours"

Ja'nell's head snapped back. She gave him a quick up and down look from behind the glass then blurted "I made my decision as well and you can stop asking if I'm going to be here or not. I'm here and I'm not going anywhere."

"I'm just letting you know."

"Thank you. Has Finnerty received the trial date yet?" She asked moving on before she became upset.

"Exactly one week from now."

"Okay well you start preparing for that and try not to worry about Janiya so much, you did all you can do for her." She made sure he heard her before asking "is there anything you need me to do out there?"

"Poke around on the nigga whose getting in Lil Ronnie way and if you come up with anything helpful put Lil Ronnie on it asap."

Standing after kissing him through the glass Ja'nell walked out of the jailhouse visiting area ready to fulfill his order.

$$$

"Ahhh...yes Brad, Oh Yes right there!" Pawlowski's bed frame was created without an actual headboard. The queen size double breasted mattress sat firmly against the wall as she panted and moaned out her past frustrations. They had been going at it for a while. Starting at first with her bent over the bed with her hands pressed into the mattress. His rhythm driving into her powerfully. Each thrust plowing into her like a wrecking ball. His muscular thighs springing her body forward whenever they banged into one another. Needing it just the way she asked of him, Pawlowski threw herself backwards meeting him in the middle; however her body still found its way itching forcefully up the bed. Before long Pawlowski had moved from the foot to the middle and was now at the head of the bed.

Sweaty with her head crammed against the wall Pawlowski moaned and begged and cried for more. Brad's hands had grown strong. Grabbing, pulling and pinching her breast. Then her hair was snatched, pulling her from the wall but his prick, that hard tan missile, seemed to challenge his grip. Loving it, Pawlowski found ways to fight for more. Her body climaxing, releasing the last bit of her frustrations before a growl from Brad came near her ear.

"EERrrrghhH!" He came. Showering her with his semen.

Too drained to see where he'd emptied his liquid Pawlowski stayed where she was and regathered her breathing. When she finally had the energy to turn over she turned to Brad coming through the door with a hot rag.

"Here" he said, matching her breathing.

Reaching for it Pawlowski snatched it out of his

hand sucking her teeth "You could have wiped for me cheap ass." She said before settling the hot cloth between her legs to calm down.

Moving as if he didn't hear her, Brad came and sat on the bed. "I was beginning to think you had lost it. You've been out of there for a while." He said referring to her absence at work.

"Things hasn't been that good so I've been laying low."

"And what about now?" He asked.

"Now I'm fine." She assured "How have you been?"

"Considering I didn't get the promotion you promised the basement hasn't been bad."

"All is not lost Brad, I believe there's still hope."

Seeing him turn to face her, Pawlowski removed the cloth and sat up. "So this call wasn't just you missing me?"

"Yes, but I've also been thinking and talking to someone, and that person thinks I should continue."

"Detective Greene?"

"Yes"

"With what. The news about your boss isn't good. No one in the department will help you and Slate probably won't even hear your presentation."

"We don't need anyone's help and I'm not presenting anything to him. Not yet."

"What do you mean we?" She heard him ask.

"Brad, you've been the only other person near this case. You know the truth behind it so you can't turn me down."

"Whenever you're suggesting free work I can."

Offended Pawlowski poked her breast out leaning closer to him. "Really" she said "You'd actually say that?"

Brad's eyes couldn't help but fall to her juggs. He felt his mouth watering all over again "What's your plan?" He asked.

"The pictures you took, do you still have them?"

"Yes but didn't you say they were worthless?"

"That was before things went to shit. Besides we're starting fresh."

"Okay" Brad said, surrendering with his hands moving to her thighs. Welcoming his touch Pawlowski laid back and opened her legs. When he pushed she grabbed a hold of his body and held him tight.

"Fuck me." She told him loving the way he felt.

CHAPTER 13

Her uncle had become an instant presence in Eclipse life. From the moment she left Eclipse in Hazik's care the two had closed the gap of unfamiliarity and became inseparable. It had been more than a week and twice' Marcey called to intervene but Hazik would not have it, however today neither was she as she came through the door of her uncle's shop.

"Hello, my two beautiful men." She interrupted finding Eclipse and Hazik both busy at work.

Eclipse was the first to pop his head up and with more energy than she'd ever remember he came running at her. "Mommy!" He shouted his arms hugging around her thighs.

Marcey smiled and hugged him back before walking over to the counter where Hazik was still glued to his work. "How are you this evening?" He asked.

Marcey watched him pick through diamonds with a magnifying glass before exhaling. "Missing my child. What have you two been up to?" She asked.

Eclipse, still filled with energy, was about to spill but Hazik caught him. "Hush boy. Never tell what you have done with your uncle and if someone ask what do you say?" She heard Hazik ask with both of them looking at Eclipse for a response.

"We had fun!" Eclipse cheered not realizing that his great uncle was installing game inside him.

"Is that all?" Marcey asked before adding "where did y'all go?"

"Nowhere." And then he nodded, laughing at his uncle.

Shaking her head Marcey shared the laughter then made her way behind the counter. A few seconds after she watched Eclipse run off to continue whatever he was doing she looked at her uncle's work in silence. "What is it, Marcey?" She heard him ask without looking at her. She stalled for a minute. Contemplating on evolving him before looking back at Eclipse collect trash around the shop. A full week had gone by since her attempt at reaching Spazz. So far he would not pick up the phone and she had no idea where he lived. The frustrations were building and despite her walking through the shop looking beautiful she was worried beyond measure. "Spit it out." He pushed.

"I messed up big time and I'm afraid of where it's going." She admitted using very small breaths as she spoke.

Putting the magnifying glass down Hazik looked at her "Not another situation." He said before asking "does it involve Lil Ronnie?"

"It's nothing Lil Ronnie has done. No."

"Explain" Hazik told her, becoming pissed.

Breathing to relax herself she said "Before Lil Ronnie went in we had another fight about his other women."

"Which you and I have talked about."

"Yes and Lil Ronnie and I have worked it out since, but at the time I was upset and we parted ways. I found someone else during that time."

"So what is the problem, Marcey?"

Quietness. She played with her hands for sometime then said fuck the stalling "the guy now wants Lil Ronnie dead and the guys friend has been keeping our product on the streets."

Hazik skin flamed but he spoke calmly "and now you're afraid Lil Ronnie will find out?"

"No Lil Ronnie knows. But he told me to end it..."

Seeing that should have been the end of the problem Hazik said "and...by the look on your face you're not?"

"I can't."

"Why?"

"Because" Marcey said "Now Tima knows and has intercepted."

This made Hazik stand. His hands went to his pockets but not with its usual smoothness. His legs took a lap around the small quarters before stopping. "Explain so I have insight on this." He said and Marcey explained the same as she did with Lil Ronnie but included the part of Tima and Nageme showing up at her home. When she was done she saw Hazik nod to say he got it.

"This won't be an issue." He stated with confidence.

"Why not? This is his way of rebelling on us and I don't think he'd listen." She said.

"No he's not going to listen but that doesn't mean we don't try. Further, your uncle has no mind for business. He has and always will be an enforcer."

Marcey heard him but so far the conversation had no promise, she needed an out. "They're going to kill Lil Ronnie and try to use his space. Uncle, I can't allow that to happen."

"Then go out there and fix this."

"But Tima is-"

"He's nothing! Marcey, don't you see your position. You are the brain of our family now and Lil Ronnie is your partner anybody in the way of that you eliminate by outsmarting them." Hazik shouted.

"Somebody can get hurt. That person could be

Tima."

"Death is a terrible result but the consequences of going against family is his fault. Do what you must but first let me have a word with him myself."

Marcey got herself together while looking at her son. She would be too busy to take him. There was extremely too much going on so instead she kissed her uncle and told her son to behave. Hazik was right. He was always right but still, as she got in the car Marcey realized Spazz not answering was still her blockage.

"Pick up, pick up" she started back pleading and cursed when the call went to voicemail. Another attempt and another and then "Spazz! Wait! do not hang up, I'm sorry okay." Her voice said in a rush. Excited he had picked up.

$$$

The backyard of his and Tay's home had a similar view to the home he was raised in with Ma Anne. The only differences were theirs were a bit bigger and instead of looking at Seacrest the interstate faced them. I95 was so close you could feel the weight when eighteen wheelers sped by. A lot of times whenever the time was given Lil Ronnie found himself in one of the lawn chairs listening to the vehicles pass. This morning was one of those times.

Kicked back holding a burning cigar, Lil Ronnie dumped the ashes into a custom designed ashtray Tay had ordered from across seas. She was lying comfortably on top of him sleeping with what once were their drinks beside them. The traffic flowed through his ears like music. Every tire engine and pipe sounded like tunes from a piano. The privacy helped him meditate allowing him to recap his week with a clear head. Besides, closing down the park and getting at Spazz he'd managed to get business flowing. There was a slight change to his operation however. Mr. Lane and Big Blue were the only ones he'd communicate with. The park with the other being shut down kept Mr.Lane busy but he had his workers so there was no worry. Big Blue had other parts of the city. He controlled his team and anyone else who wanted weight and as far as Lil Ronnie was concerned there wasn't a concern.

What the switch up did was allow him more invisibility. Made him a harder target and also gave him more time with his family. The only thing that could potentially stand in his way was Derek and his partner Spazz, but soon the streets would talk or locate and remove him as well so Lil Ronnie was in no rush. The silk material on Tay's body felt good as he rubbed his hand up and down her back. It was sheer. One she walked around the room in but they were outside and the material left little hidden. Each time he rubbed, the sheer would rise showing off more of her thighs until the bottom of her ass could be seen. Loving the way she felt Lil Ronnie went under the sheer and cuffed her ass entirely "Uhmm" a small sound escaped between Tay lips waking her. Lil Ronnie did it again but this time pieces of his finger brushed the opening between her legs feeling her moistness.

He was still in his bed clothes as well and the poor brief restraint spoke for him. Tay grabbed and stroked it but did not pull him out. Lil Ronnie saw her look up and kiss him but then her head fell back on his chest. This meant something was bothering her, putting his own wants to the side Lil Ronnie held her face up to him by the chin and asked, "What's the matter, babe?"

"I'm sitting here thinking of everything you've been through." She answered.

"I thought you were asleep."

"No, just thinking."

"Aight." Said Lil Ronnie letting her speak on her own terms.

"Mel is close to starting trial and Ja'nell is handling it well but I know my sister." Tay had said after not saying anything for a while. "She's holding it all in to be strong for him and I'm proud of her but each time I'm reminded of it I think that was the same place you just were."

"Tay, I always tell you-"

"Ronnie, I know this game comes with few happy

endings but I'm human and I'm in love and I don't want anything else to happen to you." She lifted herself from his embrace and sat up glazing at the interstate. "One of our first conversations you said you were doing what you do to help your mother and yourself. That family meant everything to you and I believe you but isn't it time to get out?"

Lil Ronnie was grateful she wasn't looking at him. His expression held an insult but he washed it away in seconds. "We can't start second guessing what we do because Mel fell. This is who we are and this is what he sacrificed himself for."

"Ronnie, baby I just don't want to lose you."

"And if you do then you know what you have to do, but I've corrected some things so bet on me baby."

A laugh sputtered from over Tay's shoulder. Through the night's glow Lil Ronnie could see her shaking her head. He knew his safety meant the world to her. Knew it from the time they'd made things official. That is what made her different. Her sincerity is what always made her special. Removing his hand from her chin Lil Ronnie kissed the side of her neck and repeatedly told her she had nothing to worry about.

$$$

The phone call led Marcey right where she

needed to be. In no time she had a location and drove where he told her the instant she had his whereabouts. When she entered the room every light inside the hotel had been left on. She walked in looking around before setting her things on the coffee table. Spazz had told her he'd be there but so far there was no sign of him. Complete silence is all she heard as she made her way in the bedding area. She looked over toward the bathroom and saw the door open. The light was on and she felt an upsetting flare to her temper. Thinking he played her, Marcey turned to get out of there however his voice stopped her midway.

"Where are you going?" She heard from behind her. Stopping, she closed her eyes to regroup before turning around.

"I was about to call you." She said, noticing a gun in his hand. Ignoring it she kept her eyes on his fully clothed body until sitting on the bed removing her shoes. "Thought you were standing me up."

Spazz moved from his spot walking past her. She saw him go to the room door and look out the peephole. When he didn't see anything he opened the door and looked both ways after sticking his head out. "It crossed my mind. You made shit clear but I wanted to know why you changed your mind." He walked toward her, setting the gun by the TV.

Marcey had visions of grabbing the gun and shooting him to death but that would stop nothing.

Tima was the ultimate problem and he would continue carrying out his plan leaving her one tool less of eliminating it altogether.

"I rather not talk about it." She said, rising to her feet as he made it over to her.

"Then what other reason would you be here?" He asked.

Marcey could almost feel the heat off his hard body as his eyes beat into hers. She lowered hers after sometime then pressed her palms against his chest. "I.. I.. I" Marcey stummered but gasped quickly when Spazz jerked her by the arm Spinning her body around. His rough hands pushed her over the bed then yanked her dress up to her shoulders. Marcey's naked and pantyless ass stood out poking in the air while he wrestled his pants down. The weight of his dick touched her a few times before she felt him pushing in holding her by the waist. It was the reason she came. She hoped it led to this and took the rushed intrusion as an invite.

Her bottom lip curled into her mouth as she bit down on it feeling pain. Her fist balled with the bed linen between her fingers and she gripped and held her scream until her moisture started easing the pain. Once her juices had spilled and greased his size she released the sheets and got more into it. Her hand went under and between her legs reaching far enough to feel his balls slapping into her. It felt so good Marcey closed her eyes and started saying his name. Asking him to fuck her more. Spazz replied by gritting. His hands squeezed into her skin as their bodies flowed with his pounding. She could feel him tensing, his man stiffening harder reminding her of the last time they had sex. Not wanting him to ever cum inside her again Marcey slipped him out and started jerking him as she fell to her knees. When he couldn't take anymore his semen splattered over her breast and Spazz stepped back panting.

Marcey with her chest full of cum stayed on her knees rubbing his semen over her body. This was her game. Her show and she would play it like nothing he'd ever seen before. When he looked up and saw her still there he gathered his last bit of breath and walked straight into her mouth. Saliva drooled as she opened, letting him hit the back of her throat. He didn't know it but Marcey was at the point of letting him do just about anything he wanted to her body. She wanted it messy, him exhausted and whatever happened between them at her place forgotten. When his dick couldn't go any further, Marcey leaned against the bed, tilted her head backwards and gave him more room to push. She was almost at the point of suffocation. His dick so far in her throat she couldn't breath. However, the minute he pulled out she exhaled leaving a glob of saliva behind. There was so much spit it hung from his length but Marcey licked and sucked until her mouth engulfed his balls. Maybe it was the mess. Or her avidness. Or the tension that couldn't help but be in the room, whichever it was brought Spazz to a second burst. His legs shook and inched back from her. Marcey watched him fall back against the stand breathing heavier than before. Without getting off her knees she crawled where he was and started licking the head of him in case any semen had been left behind.

$$$

At the mansion Tima was working on his part of the agreement. Derek's was easy. All it took was a few taps on the navigation system and the drugs would be knocking at his door. His end with Spazz however was the difficult part. He was aware after the murder not only his niece but his brother would take him differently. Marcey's indifference to him he could take without batting an eye. But when it came to Hazik there was never no telling what he'd do with his power. Both he and Hazik had influences back home in Saudi but here in the US it was Hazik who held the cards, and that alone gave Hazik the edge both in the US and back home.

Walking back from the file room with Lil Ronnie's folder Tima tossed it on the sofa then took a seat beside it. A drink of his was left on the table from earlier and he gobbled it before contemplating with his forearms resting on his knees. He was so ready to kill Lil Ronnie. Been ready since the Bell mystery but Nageme was always there giving reasons to wait. Now nothing stood in his way. Nothing except the possible wrath of Hazik who could get sanctions from back home and order him to death. Tima was fearless but knew the prices of going against family and this, that price, he had to consider.

"Hmmhnnn" he groaned with thought. His hands balled into fist as they met his mouth. The skin over his knuckles became his chewing gum. The file containing all of Lil Ronnie's personal information was picked up again. He stared at it and brought himself to anger. Tricking himself to believe the family was going against him and after all these years there was finally nothing standing in his way. "Nothing!"

"Brother, what is the matter with you? I come down stairs to find you moaning and griping."

Tima looked over his shoulder to see Nageme standing there and tried to slide the file under his thigh without being noticed. "Just thoughts in my head. Why the fuck are you still awake? It's two in the morning."

"Thoughts in my head." Nageme shrugged before getting himself a drink joining Tima on the couch. "Whose file is that?" He asked.

"Someone I'm taking a look at." Answered Tima

without moving his leg. He did however look at his brother. "Are you just gonna sit here or take your drink with you to the room."

"The room but first I'm waiting to know what you're about to do with Lil Ronnie's file." Plucking it from under his thigh Nageme started thumbing through it.

"This is none of your business so don't try to talk me out of anything." Tima muttered, taking the file out of Nageme's hands.

"None of my business?" He heard Nageme repeat. "You can't do anything to him. Especially not now. Have you heard anything Hazik has said?!"

The loudness of Nageme's voice shocked not a single nerve of Tima's and since Nageme wouldn't leave fast enough he stood to do so. "I don't give a shit what Hazik has said. He's too far up that jewelry store's ass to know what's best for us."

"So that's it, you're just going to go out and kill him?"

Tima said nothing. Pulling his jacket off the hanger, he put it on then, opened the door. "You will divide this family. You, me, Hazik, Marcey neither of us will be the same. Is that what you want, Tima?" Nageme said but the only reply was a cold stare.

When Tima broke his stare the door banged behind him and he pulled out his phone, first calling Spazz to set a meeting place.

$$$

"Keep it open... That's it... don't move your hands" Spazz's voice directed Marcey to spread open her ass. Her efforts still on dismantling any wall Spazz may have had up for her so she was still in the do-whatever-to-please-him mode. Eventually he figured the depths of her willingness and wanted to see how it felt deep inside her ass hole. Inch after inch passed through her entrance until he was halfway then he sent her a vicious slap before his dick started rocking back and forth. He was in heaven. The tight fit squeezed his size and every time they moved he got a view of Marcey voluptuous ass doing the same.

Ordering her to let her ass go he continued pushing his dick in and out watching the way her ass moved without hands. The soft natural tissue of Marcey cheeks did a slow clapping motion but sped as he quickened the pace.

"Ummmmm" Moaned Marcey as his dick became wetter. Spazz looked at her looking back then propped his foot on the bed to dive further but his phone rang and he was not one to miss it.

Pulling his dick out to get the phone Spazz answered, greeting Tima by name. "We need to meet. The information you needed on Lil Ronnie is with me."

"You're trying to do this now?" Spazz asked, unable to keep his eyes off Marcey's ass still being high in the air.

"Yes now. This time is better. Tell me where you are and I'll come to you."

The order from them not to deal with Marcey crossed his mind but Spazz brushed it off. Those rules were for Derek he told himself before giving the hotel's address.

"OK we'll meet in the parking area, someone else will be joining us as well."

Not caring about the last part, Spazz got off the phone and returned to Marcey. "Who did you give this address to?" She asked as he got back into position.

"Your uncle. He's meeting me down stairs for some business but it won't be long." Seeing her drop her head into the pillow he reentered pushing himself balls deep and did not stop until his phone rang and Marcey appeared sound asleep.

CHAPTER 14

"So the entrance to the neighborhood is tricky. Then you have the actual street but as you can see it's very narrow with absolutely no room for hiding." Brad explained. Laying next to Pawlowski in bed with his laptop sitting on his lap. Visible to both of them was real time footage of Delray Shores. Brad's finger penciled each description as he spoke.

"There's a lot of traffic for such a small street." Pawlowski commented watching the screen with unblinking eyes.

"Yeah but believe it or not. This, this and this house" he pointed at different angles "seem to know every car. Knows exactly who they're selling to. When I was surveilling most of the activity came from them but little came from the house where I seen Marcey visit."

"I've seen that layout many times." Pawlowski said. "Different houses for different reasons while the main house hid the overseers." Studying the screen some more she then said "think it'd be difficult for us going back and forth?"

Brad thought for a minute. "Doing so constantly may cause suspicion especially being that it's an all black neighborhood."

"That and there being only two entrances."

"One entrance." Brad said, causing Pawlowski to throw a questioning look his way. "I know I spoke entrances in plural but if you look here at this store you'll see the side of it is littered with thugs." Giving her time to look he added "they'll never let us through without spreading word."

"Okayyy so let's focus on this one entrance." Pawlowski said, eyeing the screen some more. Analyzing different ways things could work before saying "three cars, two drivers splitting rounds."

"Mind explaining the third car?" Brad asked.

"Sure. Two we'll drive ourselves and the third as a couple which will enable us extra footage."

"I like it." Brad admitted. "When do you want to start?"

"Now" said Pawlowski, making her way out of bed.

$$$

The peaceful act of sleep lasted long enough for

Marcey to hear the door close then she raced out of bed. Spazz had mentioned her uncle and to her that meant Lil Ronnie. Not wanting to miss anything important she found something to throw on and headed carefully out into the hall. When she got there the hall was empty with both elevators to her right however, deciding the stairs were safer she stopped short of the elevator and took the staircase. Her flat sandals went down them one at a time until she'd covered all four floors and made it to the lobby.

Having to wait in the shadows of the staircase to be sure Spazz was not present, Marcey stepped out only after she was certain. Knowing Spazz had a good start ahead she predicted them already in their meeting and rushed across the lobby to catch up. The glass doors told her the coast was clear so she came out with her eyes scanning the parking area. The lot was average with two different sections to her left and right. Using her intellect she searched for the more discreet areas and located them about twenty yards out.

Spazz was the first person she spotted. His back was to her with a car blocking his lower half. A taller white guy was beside him and finally as Marcey maneuvered closer she saw her uncle standing before them looking about half their height. Their words were unclear due to hushed tones but Marcey remained where she was and relied solely on body language. Her uncle was playing host. First with an introduction that caused Spazz to shake hands with the other guy then by producing the folder. Whatever was inside garnered the look of both men as they peered at its contents. Spazz looked up and said something to Tima who then nodded and got inside of his car and left. Staying a half second longer to watch Tima drive away Marcey heard Spazz tell the other guy he'd be right back out and started in her direction.

Turning Marcey retracted her steps to the room stripped naked and got back under the covers. When the door opened she rolled, giving her best sleeping eye. "What did he want?" She asked through a yearn.

"Told you it's about business." He said walking past her changing his clothes. She saw him include his gun this time and it alarmed her to the point of sitting up.

"You're leaving?" She asked, throwing the covers off of her.

"Yeah we'll pick up when I get back don't worry." Spazz kissed her when he finished dressing and headed out.

The door slammed closed but Marcey had it open before Spazz could make it to the elevator. She too was fully dressed this time and also chose the elevator as well knowing time was against her. When the doors slid open she was exiting just as he was leaving the lobby. Time worked perfectly for her because her car was a lot closer. Racing to it, Marcey was inside fighting to get her keys out while her eyes stayed on Spazz until he got inside a van. By the time they pulled out she was ready, departing only a few cars behind.

The van drove in a straight route for the highway. The highway led to Gateway Blvd and from there they passed Lil Ronnie's grandmother's house. The area was practically in the middle of the city so nothing stood out after they left and headed north on the highway. Things didn't start forming until miles later and Marcey saw them pulling inside Lil Ronnie's mother community. They were held up at the gate. The gate keeper made them turn around and shortly later right back on the highway they went.

There was no question they were checking Lil Ronnie residences and the reason behind it was evident. Derek's words popped into Marcey's head further clarifying her suspicions. They were planning their attack. Seeing which location was best but neither was a good option. The one and final stop they did make however brought her to worry. It was Tay's place. An address no one but her family knew about. Marcey looked in the driveway and saw Lil Ronnie's G-wagon. She felt her palms become clammy. Sweat formed in her scalp as she shook her head thinking of the folder Tima passed them. Her heart begins pounding when the Van's lights shut off. For a minute she thought they would get out and attack. Being weaponless Marcey picked up her phone to warn Lil Ronnie but saw the van pulling away shortly after.

"Phew" she heard herself exhaling, calming herself as she drove off behind them. Marcey's mind was cluttered as both vehicles went in the direction of the hotel. Tonight made things more real. Tima was really going through with it and as much as it terrified her Marcey found peace and made it back to the room in time to be oiled and naked for Spazz return.

$$$

There was a loud cough coming from upstairs.

Then another and another. After waiting for so long without it stopping, Ronnie Jr crept upstairs wondering if Lisa was okay. She had been carrying on for days but each time he got near her she either ran him off or found ways to stuff her cough. Hearing her coughing again as he climbed the stairs Ronnie Jr started moving faster barging into the room finding her hunched over. His grandfather was beside her leaning close to her mouth with a bloody towel in hand. It frightened Ronnie Jr but concern for his grandmother made him keep walking until his feet were heard.

"Jr, go back down stairs you don't need to see her like this." His grandfather told him but Ronnie Jr ignored him.

"What's the matter with her?" He asked instead coming to his grandmother's side.

Pulling the towel from Lonnie's hand to hide it Lisa tossed it in the dirty clothes and tried to appear normal. "Listen to your grandfather. I'm okay baby."

Ronnie Jr's eyes moved from the clothes bin to his disheveled grandmother. "I know you're sick Grandma, its okay." He replied letting her know he was grown enough.

When she didn't protest Ronnie Jr got close enough to hold her hand and listened at his grandfather talked to her "Lisa, you have to take these meds please."

"I can't swallow them Lonnie, y'all just give me a few it will blow over."

"No it won't. All you doing is weakening your system."

Ronnie Jr listened for as long as he could then started looking around the room. The pills Lonnie was referring to were on the bed beside her and without either of them noticing he picked them up. Leaving them to argue he went downstairs where the blender was and started one of the smoothies he saw his mother make for Ty'reek. With the blender still going he dumped two pills inside and returned to his grandparents still fighting. Walking between them Ronnie Jr asked Lisa to drink it and didn't move until she started. Halfway through the smoothie he went to get a fresh towel soaking half of it with warm water. Lisa was just finishing the glass by the time he handed her the cloth and immediately she started wiping at her neck and face.

Seeing things were under control he heard Lonnie leave and Ronnie Jr climbed next to her in bed. "Are you dying, Grandma?" He asked, looking at her.

A beautiful smile came from Lisa's tired stricken face. She looked at him, seeing the young man in him glad he was her grand baby. "You sure you want that answer?" She asked back and he nodded letting her know he was sure.

Lisa's smile went away. "Your father was around your age when we had this talk. Only he was preparing for who you see him as now...." Hearing her take a deep breath Ronnie Jr listened to Lisa start giving him the complete package. The news was beyond his age but he soaked it up until she had had enough of explaining for the day. When Lisa felt ready for a nap she made him promise not to speak a word of what he saw to his father. In turn Ronnie Jr made her promise she'd drink three smoothies a day.

$$$

Deciding to pair up on the first trip Pawlowski chose a shoulder length hairstyle that was seen on an everyday white woman. A little make up was included along with motherly earrings and one of her pearl necklaces. The authority appeal had been traded for a soccer mom's resemblance leaving her completely uncomfortable. Behind the wheel Brad drove with no problems at all. His youth alone made him fit in but for further effect he wore a ball cap without sunglasses. The two of them together screamed mother and son or worse a cougar sporting a day with her young stud. Pawlowski could care less and it showed by the way her focus stayed on the passing homes and the camera clutched in her hand.

"Where the hell is all the activity we seen on earth map?" Pawlowski asked after seeing no one.

"Oh I forgot to tell you. This is how it is here, flooded one minute and deserted the next. But they're never to far away and if you look closer at the homes I pointed out you'll see some of them sitting in windows."

Changing her focus Pawlowski saw it almost instantly. Easing her camera up she took pictures just because. "What do you think they're looking for?"

"Us!" Brad laughed. "and that." He added pointing at a stopping car. When Pawlowski looked, several individuals rushed the car from all sides. They all came from different houses but had appeared from nowhere. Easing her camera back up, Pawlowski took more pictures then looked ahead as Brad started speaking again.

"If you didn't notice none of those guys came from the main house which we are approaching now." His pinky finger pointed at the house as it appeared and Pawlowksi disregarded her camera this time.

She looked at the off-whiteness the home used as a coat matching it to the many photos Brad had already shown her. "It looks smaller." She commented before adding "whose vehicles are those?"

"The trailblazer belongs to the big couple and the Tahoe belongs to someone else. It's there on and off."

Nodding, Pawlowski got a lasting look at the Tahoe then sat back as they left the neighborhood.

CHAPTER 15

Standing in the utility room with the door closed Derek stared at twenty-four kilos of pure coke. He had just finished stacking them neatly inside the wall but couldn't come to place the sheetrock over it. Not yet at least. He was afraid the dope would disappear. Someone would snap their fingers and his dream would vanish so to save the image he just stood there in awe. This act had been carrying on since morning and for once he was not worried about Tima and Spazz's other plans.

Getting over his wave he finally reached for the sheetrock and covered the hole. Sliding the washing machine in front of it. Derek then walked out finding Sabrina and Beatup on the couch glued to the television.

"Beatup" Derek called, gaining their attention. "Put word out and let's see how fast we can move this shit."

Climbing right to his feet Beatup dug out his phone and started making calls. "You want me to fill the other houses while I'm at it they'll be calling soon."

"Yeah do that." Derek told him before getting a call himself. Seeing it was Tima, he picked up with all smiles. "My man!" He greeted.

"Ahh your voice tells me your spirit is better. No more worries aye?" Tima asked.

"Nawl no worries. My hands are full and I'm focused solely on distribution."

"Good... Spazz is coming along as well. He's partnered with someone and that problem should be over soon."

The happiness Derek felt started to wobble. Taking a deep breath he tried to talk past the bullshit. "I should be through with these in a few days, week top's."

Tima didn't give a response at first. The phone was silent and then Derek heard. "My brother Nageme always looks for the clean route. Can never make a sound decision on his own however, is that how you are Derek?" Tima asked, taking him further away from his joy.

"Yo, I don't know man, maybe. But you guys got

that end so I don't need to hear about it." Derek reminded.

"Remember your team and remember stay away from Marcey."

Saying just about anything to get off the phone Derek hung up and flopped in the chair. "You looking like you hate that muthafucka, what's up dude?" Beatup asked him.

"Shit man I don't know. This nigga suppose to be a boss but move like a fucking soldier. The only thing he's done right is dropped off this work, priority wise he's fucked up tho'" Derek rattled in frustration.

"Don't even trip. Like you say he's dropping this work off, fuck the rest."

Shaking his head he sees Beatup walking outside to meet someone and once again remembers the bigger means. He had work, his family was good and that's all that mattered.

$$\$\$\$$$

"There you go... nice..." Pawlowksi's tongue stuck half out of her mouth as her car stopped just in time to see Beatup coming outside. An old Bonneville was waiting for him and he leaned in the passenger window holding conversation. She was watching carefully. The encounter seemed like a drug deal or at least she hoped but so far there was no transaction. When movement came it was of them shaking hands through a window and she was about to become less enthused seeing Beatup head back inside. But the car stayed. The passenger's window remained down and just when she got her camera ready, Beatup came back out. This time one of his hands was filled. Something wrapped in a towel was passed through the window then, Beatup shoves money in his pocket. Her camera was snapping. Pawlowski's pictures followed him until he disappeared inside. The Bonneville pulled away and after several minutes of no action so did she. Happy she radioed Brad letting him know it was his turn.

$$$

Sitting back comfortably in his yard, Big Blue enjoyed the breeze while things flowed around him like normal. The grill was burning letting out meaty fumes and behind that thick smell was an ever louder smell of weed and liquor. A heavenly day' he'd call it, standing over the grill listening to a few of his friends go from topic to topic.

Pete and Rambo did most of the talking but Steve Mike and Sleek would chip in whenever one of the two said something that made sense. For the past ten minutes no one spoke except the two until Big Blue turned after closing the grill's door. "It's hot as a muthafucka out here today." He said going over to his seat where his towel and drink were.

"That's because you over that steamy ass grill. Sit down for a minute that meat will be aight." Said Rambo inhaling the thick blunt he'd rolled to a nub.

Big Blue turned to tell him he was right but the glitter of a brand new Benz caught his eye. He stood erect watching the car stop in front of his yard but didn't move. "Muthafucka!" He grumbled under his breath when the driver's window came down. He peeked at the windows of his house making sure his wife wasn't watching before speed walking to the car preparing to snap.

"Veronica! the hell you trying, girl?" He asked soon as his body leaned in the window.

"Nothing Daddy, I was just over here and wanted to thank you again for the car." Veronica smiled and Big Blue dropped his head. Her Alicia Key's braids and arched brows fucked him up. "Did I do something wrong?" She asked tooting out her lips.

"Nawl" he said, picking his head up but his eyes only circled her wide hips. "This just wifey spot and we don't do messy ya'dig?"

Veronica nodded but raised her leg enough to show the split in her skirt. The deep split opened intentionally and if that wasn't enough she raised the tail end and started fanning herself. Hood Bitch flashed all through her antics but they both knew he loved the shit out of it. "I hear you but what am I supposed to be doing while you over here playing house?" She asked then glanced at the other guys in his yard suggestively.

"Any muthafucking thing but that!" Big Blue snapped before going in his pocket. "Listen go do some shopping and by night fall I'll be there." Hearing her laugh as she pulled away Big Blue waited for his temperature to go down then made his way back in the yard.

"Blue, I almost thought that was the nigga Spazz's car." Said Pete just after Big Blue had sat down.

"Be a while before you see that. They shot that muthafucking car up!" Sleek said comically.

"Yeah ya boy knows how to put down I tell you that." Pete admitted to Lil Ronnie. "Streets say he wanted east side park shutdown and that bitch is now closed indefinitely." He laughed.

"Derek always been alright tho' I wonder what made him choose an out of towner." Steve cut in.

"Nigga what you mean outta towner? Delray and Boynton is damn near together!" Spoke Rambo looking at Steve like there was a problem.

"Awww nigga!" Shouted Pete. "Cause you from there doesn't mean you have to defend Delray. You know we be waring." Pete joked, making them all laugh. Big Blue however looked at Rambo almost forgetting he was from there. The first thing that came to his mind was what Lil Ronnie had asked. Acting on it immediately Big Blue stood then walked to the grill calling Rambo over for privacy.

"You know a bag is on that boy address." Informed Big Blue speaking so only the two of them heard.

Rambo, just as black as Big Blue himself, shook his head. "Hell nawl I didn't know but what are you asking?" he asked.

"I think he's still living in your city and need to know if you can get that. Lil Ronnie don't forget who fuck with him. Good graces could go a long way feel'me?"

Rambo took his time thinking about the offer but Big Blue knew the answer before the question was asked. Why; because money was superior in the hood and niggas jumped at it's every opportunity. As he guessed, a change came in Rambo's eyes before Big Blue saw the head nod. Few minutes later he was calling his daughter who happened to be familiar with Spazz. When Rambo got off the phone a message was sent to him. He sent it to Big Blue and Big Blue forwarded the address to Lil Ronnie, and just like that Lil Ronnie had the address.

$$$

When Spazz returned, the sex resumed and the entire time Marcey fought from asking what he planned to do with Lil Ronnie's locations. The only thing stopping her was her knowing he would lie and the fact of things being luminous. She didn't know why they didn't pursue killing Lil Ronnie after his jeep was spotted at home but the possibility was robbery before murder. That was the clreaest thought still, Marcey being who she were needed to know facts. Thus, finding an angle he couldn't lie about and choosing her way of asking.

Scooting under the covers bringing their bodies together Marcey startled Spazz out of his sleep by grabbing his hand pulling it around her. "How did you know I'd choose you?" She asked, speaking low and melodic.

"Look at us." He said rubbing her body. "We are meant for each other. We're both dominant but have what it takes to tame one another." He said sleepily.

"But you were sure Lil Ronnie qualities weren't the same."

"That's because he's a lil boy for real. The nigga's a lame who lucked up on a plug, you just needed me to make that shit clear to you."

Marcey said nothing. All of her disagreements

were left in her head but to get to what she needed to ask she found a way to go along with him.

"Guess you're right. Sometimes what we think is best isn't. Thank you, babe." She rolled over to kiss him pressing her breast to his chest.

Hearing him give her his welcome Marcey let a lil time pass before getting closer. "You got me but you're still after Lil Ronnie, why?"

"I thought you didn't want to talk about this shit anymore." She heard him say becoming agitated.

"I did, I needd that moment to be for us only, now I'm laying here trying to puzzle all these pieces and it's frustrating me." Taking a dramatic breath Marcey stressed "I need to know if you're here for me and the more I know the more comfortable I can be."

The sound of a deep inhale came from him as well. Intentionally, Marcey brought her body closer to his letting him think she was being sincere. "The shit was about you to a degree aight but then he fucked up. Nigga shot up my car and tried to kill me."

Him talking made Marcey produce but hide her smirk. Those few sentences told her she was in nevertheless she continued at a safe pace. "I can never understand street beef." She claimed, adding "and now my uncle is involved and he got you with another psycho."

"Yeah I'm not digging that whiteboy. Hack seem like he done been in to many wars and shit."

Hack! Marcey smiled. She was getting further. Going deeper into her book of tricks she said "I overheard them talking, my uncle and Hack. Hack was mad about you as well. He likes working alone."

"I don't give a fuck. We don't have to say shit to each other long as that nigga is dead by the end of tomorrow." He spat and like rattling the cage of a wild animal she got him to start lashing out. Telling his plans through obvious anger. Marcey felt his chest rise and fall and caressed it. All while diving deeper in her tricks.

"The end of tomorrow? Spazz that's only a few hours away. When will I see you again?" She asked this time looking up with worried eyes.

"Don't worry I won't get missing until dark and long as you're here when I get back you'll see me."

"Okay" Marcey said with the urge to climb back on his dick. However she pushed off of him and got out of bed. There would be no more sex for them she thought as she went inside the bathroom and took a hot shower.

$$$

Like a coach receiving a special call from the

bullpen Lil Ronnie slid his message box open and scanned Spazz's address. That familiar smirk appeared over his lips before clearing the screen. The tiny bruise Spazz had given Mr Lane was a mere thought. Lil Ronnie had only sent shots from his own gun to show the out of towner nothing about him was sweet, however the individual in Spazz himself was a thought. He was teamed with Derek and was known in the streets to shoot first so with that Lil Ronnie left the presence of Tay and made a call in private. The call was answered on the second ring and he got straight to the point. "Dat birdy just dropped and I need y'all on it pronto."

"You got the addy?" Hot replied, ready to round up and move.

Telling Hot it would be forwarded soon as he got off the phone, Lil Ronnie ended the call. Suddenly he had a taste for more to drink. Pulling a bottle of liquor from the shelf he walked it over to the den and took a seat. Twelve long years he'd been in the game now and each one had zoomed quicker than the blink of an eye. Honored to say however he remembers each and every event. Every lesson, every mistake and every heart break. Remembered his excitement before getting started. The anticipation of being a hustler. Days of walking the hood aimlessly with his man Mel. All the fabricated stories Mel told. This made Lil Ronnie laugh. Reminded Lil Ronnie that those fabrications somehow came true for his man. And then he thought of Frank. Sadness tried to take over but a set of headlights flashing through the window distracted him. Looking at the State of the Art security screen he saw Ja'nell getting out of her car with bags in hand. Standing Lil Ronnie opened the door with a big smile.

"Sis, what it do?" He greeted with a fresh cup of liquor in one hand the other outstretched.

"Nothing much bro" she replied, giving him a hug before entering and putting the bags on the couch. When she was done Ja'nell spun on her toes looking around "god, I get awestruck every time I come in here."

Taking the compliment Lil Ronnie told her Tay was upstairs then went back to his seat but by the time he landed on the chair Ja'nell was at his side. "Ronnie, can we talk right quick? It shouldn't take long I promise." She said.

With the look of question Lil Ronnie nodded and told her to sit. "What's on your mind?" He asked.

Ja'nell breathed before speaking and when she did her voice trembled with uncertain boundaries. "You know I stay out of y'alls business and if it wasn't for Mel asking that's exactly what I'd be doing."

"I know" Lil Ronnie said, adding. "Just ask and we'll take it from there."

Instead of answering Ja'nell reached in her hand bag. "With all that's going on I thought maybe this could help." When Lil Ronnie looked at her hand she had a phone extended his way. Taking it he looked at the screen seeing a social media page. "Scroll up and down and you'll see photos of-"

"I got it, I got it." Lil Ronnie informed sitting up more. He looked at images of Spazz and couldn't believe all the information being displayed. "Is this recent?" He asked.

"Yep. His wife posts almost every hour. Their address is there as well."

Lil Ronnie heard her but his hand kept strolling the pictures until he came across some kids. Three of them. All boys. Something in him felt off. Rushing where she said the address would be Lil Ronnie matched it to the one he had and jumped up. "Fuck!" He uttered, snatching his phone.

"The caller you're trying to re-" Lil Ronnie hung up and dialed again. Same response. Voicemail first ring. Grabbing his car keys he rushed out hoping it wasn't too late.

$$$

More photos were taken but today the footage

was closer. Pawlowski couldn't help herself. The van the car was becoming boring and believing she could blend in she dressed down in a joggers suit strapped a hidden camera to her bicep and treated it like an MP player. The neighborhood was finally showing what she'd originally thought. People, traffic, even kids were at a full swing. Using the sidewalk that led to the main house Pawlowski jogged through her share of unwanted looks before putting sites on the trap house.

Beatup was seen standing by the trailblazer smoking a cigarette and Pawlowski made a quick decision before bringing her toned legs to a stop. Recklessly she entered the gateless yard and walked up on him.

"Aye what the fuck." Beatup said surprised. Turning to find her less than two arm lengths away from him.

Putting on her most naive look Pawlowski apologized for startling him then smiled. "I was hoping you could help me. My family and I moved here recently but haven't seen any bus stops for our kids. Do you know where they'll be?"

The glare Beatup turned to her with relaxed and then he looked out into the street. "You missed all the people with that answer. Go out there and ask them." He said pointing back out to the street.

Looking over her shoulder as though considering

Pawlowski turned back to face him. "I'm sorry they don't look as friendly as you. I'm Natalie" she went on to say while puffing out her breast and extending her hand.

Noticing her large chest, his eyes begin to linger. A quarter of a minute later his eyes finally realized the hand she had sticking out. "Can't do handshakes around here. Police will start assuming ya'dig?" He said then looked back at her breast.

Pawlowski smirked as he gawked a little but when growth appeared under his zipper she started to hope this was her way to get close to one of them. Stepping closer Pawlowski was about to ask if he liked what he saw but the house door opened and change attacked the atmosphere immediately.

"Who the hell is this, Beatup?!" Pawlowski heard a female voice shout. Pawlowski turned to see if it was the larger woman and sure enough she saw Sabrina marching over. Sabrina was at least three inches taller than her and the weight was beyond comparable. Pawlowski put some difference between her and Beatup then tried the innocent look.

"Hi ma'am" she gushed with a wave. "I just stopped to ask if-"

"No! You're about to get the fuck out of this yard. I seen your flirting ass from the window now get on!"

Deciding the woman had a short temper, Pawlowski wiped out the innocent look and walked away. Just a few seconds more and Beatup may have been eating from her palm, but all was lost because Sabrina was the distraction she needed to get close and personal pictures.

$$$

"Fuck fuck fuck fuck!!!!" Lil Ronnie hand pounded down on the steering wheel. His foot jammed the pedal to the floor but the car wouldn't move fast enough. The phone clutching inside his other hand was only making him angrier. Each attempt, same result, and he'd tried reaching all three of them. Swerving from behind one car then another Lil Ronnie zoomed past traffic. Weaving from lane to lane until reaching Atlantic Blvd, he did another hard swerve nearly causing a collision. Horns blared, brakes were used but Lil Ronnie ignored them and shot through the underpass heading east.

A red light made him glimpse at his phone again. Nothing! Frustrated and in a hurry Lil Ronnie found a small opening in the cluttered traffic and bullied his way through the light. The navigation system told him three minutes away. However, not settling, he pushed the G-wagon some more ripping through ocean avenue until the time was cut in half and he was close enough to hear gunshots if they were erupting. For the first time since leaving his home he felt himself breathing. His eyes bounced around the street as he drove but he was mainly looking for his men. No kids. No women. His mind told him. Lil Ronnie wanted Spazz but patient enough to keep it between them. His tires rode up a little more before real exhalation came and he spotted the Chevy parked further down the street. Pulling up behind them Lil Ronnie got out, tapped the back window then climbed inside.

$$$

"Who the fuck was the lady?" Asked Derek after Sabrina came inside shouting.

The door banged closed and Beatup looked at him smirking. Laughing, Derek took it as nothing but not Sabrina. Sabrina wanted to fight. "Don't laugh with him, Derek! This muthafucka out there in some white bitch face and we in here working, with his stupid ass!"

"I wasn't in the bitch face she was asking me shit now calm the fuck down already!" Beatup yelled back.

"Dat bitch wanted dick. Dope smoking ass hoe,

she know what the fuck going on round hea!"

Shaking his head Beatup went and sat down. The TV became his focus point leaving Sabrina to calm down on her on. Almost instantly Derek saw her go over to the couch where her weed was and start rolling a blunt. Derek looked at Beatup. True enough they were in the middle of the hood but no one was supposed to come there. No one should have entered the yard if they didn't approve and Derek was starting to take it more serious."You really don't know that bitch?" He asked keeping his voice between them two.

Peeking at Sabrina Beatup shook his head "Bitch was jogging and stopped to ask about a bus stop. Some about just moving here."

"You did realize she was over fifty right? Rarely you catch a age like that with kids still in school."

Looking at him Beatup shrugged "that's what the bitch said."

"He's stupid!" Sabrina jumped to her feet. They didn't even realize she could hear them but she was on point climbing back to her feet, blunt rolled. "Her white ass probably the police!"

"The lady ain't no fucking police. I would have known, Sabrina." Beatup dismissed but Derek wasn't so sure.

He had a lot of coke and money there, one fuck up could ruin it all. One fuck up and they were all back broke and federally bounded. Not wanting to overlook anything Derek walked outside and scanned every car. When nothing suspicious popped out he walked further up the street and stopped the first kid he saw. "Shorty, you stay round here?" He asked the kid.

The young boy sized him up then nodded after acknowledging his fresh clothes and jewelry. "I was wondering if any white people lived around here. Do you know any?"

The kid face contorted with humor "yep." The kid nodded "they scared to fuck with us tho'. Some live down that street. About three houses of them."

"Aight bet." Derek let the kid go and looked back over the street. Maybe he was looking too deep into shit. He considered before going back to the house, resuming his day.

CHAPTER 16

Although sex was no longer needed Marcey stayed in the room until Spazz fell asleep. It was a little after 5pm when she snuck out and even with it being risky she needed the separation to prepare herself. Speeding across town to her condo, Marcey rushed inside taking a quick shower. Minutes later she was dressed in dark spandex. Her hair pulled into a bun with her tennis shoes laced tightly. On the way out she stopped at the closet where Lil Ronnie kept one of his guns and checked the magazine. Seeing all seventeen rounds were in place she took it.

So far her plan was going well, and had become better once she arrived at the hotel's parking area hearing her phone rung. "Jackie, where are you?" She heard Spazz ask. His voice told her he was now fully awake.

"Sorry I didn't want to wake you before I left. I'm on the way to my uncles. Eclipse is driving them nuts" she joked but could hear Spazz breath with disapproval.

"Aight." He forced after some time. "I gotta get up with this shit anyway. Make sho' you're here when I get back."

Staring at the hotel from her position she said "I'm coming back soon as I have Eclipse settled don't worry."

"Cool" Marcey heard him saying but neither hung up. A shuffling noise was heard in the background which told her he was packing to leave. Then his voice came back over the line. "Aye Marcey"

"I'm here." She replied, watching the doorway.

"Don't say shit about what you heard. I'm trusting you." The hotel room door closed and Marcey started counting down for his departure.

"You should know me by now, Spazz. I've chosen and once I've decided there's no changing it." Her words meant more than what he heard but the conversation ended there just as Spazz was walking out.

Marcey watched him carry his bag to the car then get in pulling off. Taking I95 south she followed safely a few exits down then turned off until they were following the same path Lil Ronnie took earlier. His car pulled into a yard and Marcey had no clue as to who lived there. The answer came soon after when the front door opened and a woman with a baby in her hands met him outside. Spazz kissed her and the baby before two more boys came out hugging him.

Family! Marcey realized. Anger tried to seep in from a small feeling of being played but she kept her composer watching them enter the house. Not knowing how long he'd keep her waiting Marcey jacked her seat back to get comfortable and started surveying the area. Wait!! Marcey shot right back up leaning toward the windshield. "Is that?" Her voice trailed seeing the reality of what was in front of her. What was about to take place.

Crouched down one behind the other she spotted Lil Ronnie and company making their way back to the Chevy. Her heart pounded. What was he doing here? She questioned before it fully hit her. They were here for Spazz and they had him!" A bunch of thoughts crossed her mind and as they slowed she started to understand what had them backing off. Spazz, little did he know, had just been spared for the sake of his family. The tail lights to Lil Ronnie's G-wagon flashed and Marcey saw him pull off. The Chevy followed both vehicles going in the opposite direction of her. Marcey couldn't believe it. Marcey could barely breathe. Marcey sat back and waited on Spazz. He was dead and didn't even know it.

$$$

So far forty-seven photographs have been taken. Creating a pattern from old to new, Brad and Pawlowski trailed it from the time Marcey was followed to the family mansion. The next photo was of her and Derek talking in front of the trap house. Pawlowski skipped over some photos to link Marcey and Derek's to that of Beatup and Sabrina.

The bag passing between Marcey and Derek was included along with a few other photos then Pawlowski tried to form her story. "So the niece of the drug family is here." Pawlowski said, sliding Marcey's picture to the top. "Then there's Derek with what were going to assume is drugs... and these two are his workers." Then she slid in photos of the house. "This is where the drugs are delivered, held, and or distributed." She then slid in the photo of the mansion. "To sum it up all of them are working for the Rouhani family." A red marker circled the mansion before Pawlowski looked toward Brad for an opinion.

"Terrific story." He said cheerfully.

Pawlowski frowned "It's not enough. We need something for any of this to stand."

"It sounds believable to me."

"Brad, no offense but that is because you're still inexperienced. Any judge will bat it down. There has to be soundproof. Something unexplainable."

Getting up from her dining room table Pawlowski fetched some wine and tried expanding her mind. Never again would she bring in a case half assed. The consequences were humiliating, job threatening and too much of a damn waste. Pouring Brad and herself a glass she sat down in thought. "I never seen them leave much and I remember you mentioning the couple but have you noticed the Tahoe hasn't moved much either." She said thinking of Derek's vehicle.

"I've noticed. So what are you thinking?" Brad asked.

"I'm thinking their deals can't be too hidden. People that move weight usually have far less transactions but they do have them and that means we're missing something."

"Could our timing be a little off?" Brad asked.

"It's what I'm starting to consider." The wine swirled as she moved her glass. "Maybe we could go round the clock. Twenty-four hour surveillance." She said, setting the glass down.

Brad's look became bewildered "you mean an actual twenty-four hour surveillance. No there's no way I can commit to that!" He said seriously.

"Oh Brad, don't start with that. This is me asking for a favor."

"No Pawlowski, not this time. It's not going to work."

"This case will do us both some good.

Recognition for you. The reinvention of my name. The rewards are endless"

"And the sacrifice is costly. I have a job, Pawlowski."

"And so do I." She said before begging "one week is all I ask for."

Closing his mouth before any word could spill, Brad tossed his wine glass back "One week and it's back to normal."

"One week" she promised.

$$$

An hour and fifteen minutes had passed before the front door opened again. Spazz with a bag in one hand and T-shirt over his shoulder stepped out and walked to his car. Not once did his head peek up for any peril, which was the second time she considered him lucky but he did give extra support to his waistline. Seconds after he had the door open Marcey watched him pull an assault rifle from inside his pants and got into the car.

She waited until he turned off the street before pulling off behind him. Catching up just in time to see him head north on the highway she followed him exit after exit. When all the exits to Boynton had been passed she began to question his destination but Lil Ronnie called giving her something better to do.

"Hello my son's beautiful father, I was getting ready to call you."

"I guess our minds really do think alike. What have you been up to?" She heard him ask and Marcey looked at the bumper of the car Spazz was driving.

"Just the usual. Minor work here and there and you, how's business?"

"Nice" Lil Ronnie told her. She heard him go flat but in almost the same breath he asked "have you figured things out yet. You know I won't let that go."

"I know and I will, Ronnie. Tell you what whenever we see each other again we'll talk more." Making a right behind Spazz on tenth Avenue she followed him west. "Is that okay with you?" She asked

"That'll do. Call me when you make it home and I'll stop by." When he got off the phone Marcey paid more attention to where Spazz was leading her. Tiny rock pebbles were felt under her tire as he drove them into a section of trailer parks. She hoped she wasn't boxing herself in but continued driving until Spazz stopped and she saw Hack's van parked at one of the trailers.

As if on cue Hack came out with a different kind of assault rifle and slid the side door open. Both of them put their guns in then walked to the front. When they drove off Marcey started to feel her adrenaline. Time was nearing and she was indecisive toward its ending.

CHAPTER 17

The sky had just fallen to it's pitch blackness by the time Lisa and Lonnie made it halfway around Plam Beach Lake trail. The trail was about five miles long, a lengthy stretch for someone in her health but the smoothies Ronnie Jr made her worked like energy drinks. Within weeks Lisa was back pumping and moving better than her old self. Ronnie Jr did not let his little mind rest at the energy drinks. He created an entirely new routine for them. Made fitness a top priority, got all of them to agree and become committed to his exercise plan. Since their talks he had been very clear about her health and had studied exercises that worked directly with the immune system. Case in point, they were gonna do whatever it took to extend his grandmother life and she was his number one supporter.

Without breaking a stride Lisa heard her phone

ringing and without having to look knew who was calling. . "You're late, sugar" She answered breathlessly.

"I know." Ronnie Jr said. "Ty'reek was misbehaving. Have you started your walk?" He asked.

"Almost finished. Me and your grandfather will be home shortly. Did your father make it out with y'all tonight?"

"No, not yet. He's been out all day."

"Was he home?"

"Yep. On the couch."

"Well okay sugar, next time don't take no for an answer. We'll talk later okay." Hearing him agree Lisa ended the call and pumped her arms harder while thinking of how blessed they all were. They're lives seemed fit for battles. Battles most people lost but not them. They were built off love and bonded by care. Lonnie took a loud breath causing her to look his way and Lisa laughed seeing him barely holding on. "We're almost there baby, one more mile."

"I ain't quitting." Were the first words he said under a pour of sweat. Forever the weakest link Lonnie was the only one of them all who fought to accomplish the five mile walk. Lisa didn't mention it however, she just enjoyed his company.

"I know you're not baby, you're doing great." She said slowing to help his pace.

"Thanks. Now talk about something else."

Laughing, Lisa knew he was trying to take the walk off his mind. "Alright then..." She said thoughtfully "How about a cookout. What you think of that?"

"How about one step at a time. You just got back into the swing of things and I don't need you pushing it." He said, holding his head high for oxygen.

The fire in Lisa made her want to challenge him but figured she'd been doing too much of that lately. "You're the man. I'll plan whenever you're ready." Her voice settled cheerfully.

Completing the rest of their walk in silence they made it to the car relieved and satisfied. Lisa looked up at the sky watching it cover in darkness. The clouds seemed thicker and darker. The night became still and something at the pit of her stomach made her send up a prayer for her and her family.

$$$

The van drove south until reaching Gateway then took the right turn on seacrest. The van was a Mini Quest with a midnight paint. Its tires were spray painted black, making it almost impossible to see at this hour. Inside the van Spazz had Hack's CR-56 machine gun turning the high powered rifle over in his hands. "Aye, I don't mean to get in your business and shit but where the fuck you get something like this?"

Looking from behind the wheel, Hack glazed at Spazz ready to get the job over and done with. Knowing the feelings were mutual however he went along with the small talk. "That's a puppy compared to the arsenal I have at home."

"I bet. What kind of bullets you putting in here?"

"Same ones you put in an AK-47 but it's American mad so the velocity is a lot more dependable."

"Sounds like you done used this big muthafucka before."

Hack smiled. His smile however was unpleasant with coffee and tar stains all over his frontal teeth. "People like the Rouhani's don't hire me because I'm white. I was passed around from job to job since my early teens. Never fucked up never missed nor do I plan to." The statement splattered like an insult. Looking at the white guy in the dark interior almost made Spazz say some fucked up shit. Instead he thought about Marcey words regarding the way Hack felt about him and nodded mockingly.

"Yeah aight Rambo, we're about to see that shit in a minute." He said, putting the gun back and picking up his own checking the clip.

"See that gun alone tells me you're a rookie." Hack said then reached over, taking it from him. "It's not even set at fully auto. The most you'll get is a three round burst. I'd have chosen a hand gun instead."

Snatching his gun, Spazz told Hack to watch it. He couldn't wait to get the show on the road. He was gonna show Lil Ronnie and this muthafucka beside him.

$$$

As the van drove ahead of her Marcey did a process of eliminations until she knew for sure they were headed back to Tay's place. The ETA was about two minutes out and Marcey did not like it. Did not like the danger coming around Lil Ronnie's family but, her uncle's acquisitiveness over road anything reasonable. The gun she'd got from the closet was a Sig 9mm. Very light in weight with barely any kick. Taking it out the bag she placed it on her lap thinking of the weaponry they held.

Standing in a head on gun battle with them was suicidal. They're fire power would swarm her in seconds. She knew that the instant she saw both their rifles, therefore a little disturbance is what she sought.

Waiting for them to turn into the neighborhood, Marcey took a short cut and rounded Tay's street for layout. Scanning the houses and vehicles nearby she found what she was looking for then floored it to the next street over. Her trained eyes combed the homes before locating the right one then got out of her car. Shielding the gun close to her body Marcey crossed the lawn climbed a small gate then came out between another house. This house is the one she'd picked on Tay's street. The one that positioned her directly across the street. Satisfied with her position she took a seat in the homeowner's lawn chair then sat back watching for the van.

$$$

To Eclipse the mansion was like a maze but there were no tight corners or zig zags. There were instead circular stairs and many doors. Trying to take it all in Eclipse little feet kept spinning and spinning until hearing Hazik chuckle from across the room. "Eclipse, you're spinning like a mary-go-round. Move. Go anywhere you want." Hazik said. Looking at him from the foyer Eclipse did not move. It wasn't the same as the shop and being there this time was different without his mother. Eclipse eyes kept bouncing over different areas of the house uncomfortably until Hazik got enough and came over.

"Okay." He heard his uncle say. "I'll show you around once and then you are on your own." The tour took him everywhere. Each of their rooms, family rooms, patio, even the camera room. When they were on their way downstairs, Eclipse noticed a photograph he had seen on the way up and pointed toward it. "That is the entire family." Hazik smiled, picking him up for a closer view. "Do any of them look familiar?" He asked of the twenty plus people in the photo.

"That's you" Eclipse pointed first after a close look at the picture.

"That's correct and whose this?" He asked.

"Uncle Tima."

"And here?"

"Uncle Nageme." Eclipse smiled.

"Okay smart guy, tell me who are these two people." Looking at the picture Hazik pointed out a man holding an infant, Eclipse took his time. The faces didn't seem too familiar to him but still he tried until an absolutely blink expression crossed his face. "That tiny little insect is your mother and that's your big pop." Informed Hazik.

"Where is he?" Eclipse asked with lit eyes.

"Dead." Hazik admitted sadly. "Your grandfather was like us, warriors in the streets of Arabia. He'd killed more than one hundred and fifty people before our rival caught him."

Silence took on as Eclipse digested what he'd heard. Hazik pointed at another picture. One right beside it and hopes to cheer Eclipse back up. "You see this one. The head under my right foot?" Eclipse nodded. "That was the man responsible. Not long after we ran into their village and slaughtered everyone. It was my first beheading." Putting him down Hazik said "Not much about this family is spoken in pride. We were raised differently than those of this country. Drugs, money and murder is our breed and that may be what you are.

"Can we go visit there sometime?" Eclipse asked.

"Inshallah we'll travel in the near feature." Replied Hazik, speaking with humility.

As they made it down stairs and walked into the den things changed. Hazik became very tense and the voice he used with Eclipse was no longer present.

$$$

The van appeared just after Marcey sat down. She watched it pass for a look before reversing finding a parking space on side of the road. Marcey noticed how the location Hack placed the van was for an unnoticeable getaway, but for a while neither door opened. Then both opened at the same time. Their tall bodies scanned the area with their eyes before creeping into Tay's yard using Lil Ronnie's G-wagon to hide behind. Marcey looked at the house. Inside was a well lit interior but so far no movement had passed by the windows. Peeking at Spazz and Hack's position, Marcey got up from the chair then crouch-walked as close as she could without being noticable.

Her head whipped toward the top of the street.

Voices were heard coming down. Different pitches of tones. Adults as well as kids and something about them made Marcey stay focused in the direction. Almost simultaneously to her peeking a child dashed out into the street causing another to run after him. The little bodies were only outlines at first, but then Marcey gasped. "Shit" she said beneath her breath recognizing Ronnie Jr. She watched him pull his brother back to safety but her eyes were now moving frantically. They were only a few houses away. Spazz and Hack were already at their house. Marcey mind fast forwarded to what Hack or Spazz would do to them once they entered the yard. The thought was not good, and she immediately begin looking for a diversion. Another house closer made Hack pick up the noise as well. He looked toward the family and tapped Spazz who also looked in the direction and as if they knew who the family belonged to she saw Hack turn in their direction. Marcey felt her heart racing. She looked down at her gun still pondering on the correct diversion. When she looked back up she saw Hack ready to confront the family and knew taking them hostage meant forcing Lil Ronnie out and in the open. Wanting neither to happen, Marcey got as low as she could to the ground, aimed her gun and started counting. One...two...three... By the time she got to five they were only a house away and having no other option she fired, sending a bullet zipping across their path. Tay and another woman grabbed the kids and tried to run for the house but Marcey fired again. This shot made them all drop however Marcey shifted her gun back on Hack before they could hit the concrete.

Hack eyes keyed in on where the shots came from but Marcey moved before he could spot her position. The high beams to Tay's lawn flooded the yard putting Hack and Spazz on front street. She glanced at the house once more and spotted Lil Ronnie. The gun shots made him alert. With his gun in hand Lil Ronnie spotted his two intruders and wasted no time pulling the trigger, wrecking havoc.

$$\$\$\$$$

"What in the fuck do you call yourself pulling?" Shot Hazik, his eyes turning bloodshot as he realized Tima was inside the mansion.

Barely moving his head from the television Tima looked at Hazik standing there with Eclipse by his side. Guessing Marcey had run her mouth he said nonchalantly, "I'm doing what should have been done. This family doesn't need Lil Ronnie's services any longer." Dismissively he turned back to the soccer game he was watching.

Feeling blood rush through his body, Hazik walked where the remote was lying on the table and clicked off the game.

"Nagme" Hazik yelled from downstairs and then waited patiently for his arrival. "Take Eclipse with you upstairs please." When the sounds of their feet disappeared upstairs Hazik started rolling up his shirt sleeves. "Doing what should have been done?" He repeated finishing on the last sleeve. "So this family is under your authority now. Is that what the fuck you're telling me?" Hazik asked before shouting "Get the fuck up!"

Tima, known as the more violent one, smiled at his brother. Both of them were closing in on their sixties but no one could have reminded them of their ages today. Climbing to his feet with that same smile Tima asked, "Now what, you're gonna fight me over a burnt piece of nigger skin? He's no fucking good to us. The people I have-" is the farthest Tima got before a loud roar came from Hazik. Charging his brother with all his speed Hazik caused them both to go flying over the back of a couch.

Strapping to get to the top position the lighter and faster weight of Hazik's won and as soon as both knees were planted on either side of Tima's body he sent a striking closed fist to his jaw. Another came behind it but Tima blocked and used his weight rolling Hazik onto his back. A gut shot was delivered to Hazik midsection. Tima's forearm then came down hard under Hazik's chin, shorting any of his air supply. As a survival Hazik started kicking his feet digging into the plush carpet until catching grip forcing Tima off of him. Winded Hazik climbed to his feet, took a deep breath and crashed his body into Tima's again. For the second time they came down hard to the floor with Hazik landing on top. "Come on!" Hazik shouted. "You want to challenge me! You think you can wear my fucking shoes!!" Hazik screamed, taking a hold of Tima's head, banging it into the floor. The sounds of his brother's head knocking dangerously beneath him echoed warnings of death but his rage understood one thing. Death. And it was vastly becoming the goal.

$$$

Thutt thutt thutt thutt thutt - bullets flew - Marcey ducked even when no barrel was aimed her way. You could hear loud sounds of metal clanking as bullets ripped through Lil Ronnie's G-wagon. From where she was the reverberation of firepower came from everywhere. Only when she was certain the projectiles were not for her did she lift her head peeking at the yard. Bullets and sparks flew from Lil Ronnie's G-wagon and Marcey looked back at the house noticing Lil Ronnie was the only active shooter. When she looked over for Spazz and Hack positions they were crowded low on the other side of the G-wagon waiting for Lil Ronnie to run out of rounds. Marcey kept her eyes trained on them predicting when they would take their chance. It came as soon as her prediction occurred. Lil Ronnie stopped to reload and Hack stood to attack but a couple shots from her gun forced him back down.

"Dammit!" Travel from their positions. "There's two shooters!" She heard Hack yell, pointing across the street then to the upstairs open window Lil Ronnie shot from. Marcey ducked out of view but held visual by looking under a car. She saw Spazz and Hack speak back and forth then at the exact same time Spazz rose firing at the upstairs window while Hack fired in her direction. The bullets weren't even close to hitting her. Hack was shooting blindly as well as Spazz but as Marcey looked back underneath the car she found Lil Ronnie outside moving toward his enemies. Gun battle started again but Marcey had to shift her vision to a moving Hack coming her way. His feet took him to the last area she'd been spotted and that proved to be a severe mistake. Knowing where his next step would lead him, Marcey rose to one knee and aimed.

$$$

Bang-Bang-Bang! Hazik assault was continuing. He felt Tima's hands try prying his hands away but Hazik was committed to killing his own blood and would have if it wasn't for someone rushing over tackling him off of his brother. When Hazik looked to see what happened he saw Nageme standing with his face red and filled with anger.

"We are family!" Screamed Nageme. His cheeks flushing each time they flared with hot air. "And you two are acting like idiots!"

"He is the fucking idiot. Go against everything I fucking say as if I didn't put us here!!" Seeing Tima getting to his feet, Hazik tried rushing through Nageme but failed.

"Fuck you!" He heard Tima say, checking the back of his head for blood. Relieved none was there he stated "You expect us to stand by while you let this nigger fuck over this entire family. You're no leader, never has been and from here own you dictate nothing!"

"You will suffer without my leadership. You know little of this country but think you have it all figured out." Hazik took small breaths to cool down but stayed on the ready.

"We'll see" Promised Tima, grabbing his keys to leave.

"You walk out that door, your blood is no longer protected. This family, this house, no longer welcomes you and you can find your own transport for this months shipment." Making it as clear as he could Hazik watched Tima leave. They were brothers and if any of them cared about family it was him so seeing even his most hated brother walk out hurted. Going to take a seat on the couch Hazik put his head down and just sat for a while.

The touch of Nageme hand falling on his shoulder pulled him from his state but more than anything it was Nageme's next words

"You have done wonderful as the middle brother and Tima has wanted this since you became leader. Don't worry." Nageme was about to walk off then stopped "If it helps anything Lil Ronnie could be under attack right now and even if he make it through Tima will not stop."

"What the fuck is the matter with him?!" Hazik fumed. His anger ascending once more.

"I don't know but this guy Derek was his missing piece and with him Tima can do what he has with Bell or so he thinks."

Watching Nageme walk off, Hazik pulled out his phone warning Lil Ronnie. He then sent a more urgent message to Marcey. Informing her Tima was now an enemy.

$$$

Hack steps were lite and steady and calculative but none of that helped when Marcey doubled tapped her trigger hitting him in the chest and torso. The impact caused Hack's rifle to slip halfway out of his hands but somehow he managed to hold the trigger sending wild rounds to the ground. Chunks of cement flew up and Marcey was tempted to give him more but couldn't risk exposure. Instead she kept the car for cover watching Hack cuff his wounds while backpedaling to safety.

Each time his hand came away from his torso blood gushed making him cover it again. Still the soldier in him tried to find a way of attack but Marcey was nowhere in his sights. Struggling to turn toward the house he spotted Spazz in heated exchange but the metal that tore through his muscles wouldn't allow him the strength.

Spazz yelled for him after his gun jammed with an empty clip. Straining Hack called back out for them to retreat and as Spazz made his way over more hailing bullets from Lil Ronnie made them flee with prayer.

Marcey stood from her position. She was on the same side Lil Ronnie's family had dropped to coverage. She saw Tay huddled over them safely before darting her vision to see Spazz pushing Hack into the van. She could have finished them if she wanted. Closed the gap between them and dome checked the both of them however she knew the time would come again. The last person she saw before racing back to her car was Lil Ronnie. He was breathing heavily. His chest heaving like a warrior's who had just defended his territory.

CHAPTER 18

The phone was still in Hazik's hand when Marcey walked through the mansion's double doors. Before anyone could speak she asked for a minute then went to her old room for a shower. Although no evidence was visible Marcey felt as if the remnants of blood was all over her. Using the shower's hottest temperature to wash under, she closed her eyes replaying the night. Lil Ronnie must have really been shaken after realizing Spazz had brought drama to his home. Marcey had never seen him throwing himself in harm's way like he did tonight. It was like he completely disregarded his own life to push his assailants away from his home and to think he'd just spared Spazz and his family. This was no longer about her or a street beef. This was now personal and Marcey knew Lil Ronnie would hunt with all cards off the table.

Cutting off the water Marcey dressed quickly to get down to her uncles but made it a priority to check in on Eclipse first. Seeing him sleeping with covers pulled to his chin she closed the door then returned downstairs giving her uncles a proper greeting. "Has Eclipse been trouble?" She asked, displaying a smile that did not tell the night's events.

"Silent assassin Eclipse is. Don't remember you ever being as quiet as him." Nageme commented before Hazik cleared his throat.

"I've just received bad news did you receive my message?" Asked Hazik giving her a look that wiped her smile away.

"No" she answered, looking back at him. "Are you okay what happened to your clothes?" She added noticing Hazik's ruffled attire.

"Later about me. Lil Ronnie has not answered my messages and he could be in danger." His words made Marcey eyes climb from his clothing to his reddened eyes. She tried sending him a warning with her eyes but failed due to his anger. Giving up Marcey simply nodded toward Nageme. "Nageme is fine you can speak, Marcey." Hazik informed not missing her gesture.

Nodding she said "an attack happened but Lil Ronnie is fine. I made sure of it."

"What happened?" He asked.

"Tima gave up Ronnie's home address and a

shooting took place. I may have killed one of them." Marcey said without regret.

"Does Lil Ronnie know you were involved?"

"No" Marcey answered. "I hid my presence."

"Jesus. Where is the gun you used, Marcey?" Nageme worriedly asked.

"Destroyed it before coming here. My tracks are fine no worries." She told him.

"You did good, Marcey."

"Thank you." She told Hazik. "Now what happened to you?"

"Tima" He spat bitterly.

Now it was Marcey's turn to worry. Walking over she sat between them looking him over closely. "Tima is the one needing to be examined. God don't punish the righteous." Assured Nageme.

Soothing Hazik hair back with her hand she thought of the name they had just used and how it made her feel. "Tima... And where is he?" She asked.

Nageme stayed quiet on this one she noticed. Marcey sights went to Hazik "Don't know and don't care. Tima is no longer welcome here. The Rouhani family never turns against family and those that do become the highest of adversaries."

"He will only go harder at Lil Ronnie." Marcey informed.

"Not if you go hard on him first. Remove him from the equation and do so however is fit. The family back home has been advised."

Her eyes checked for Nageme. Nageme nodded and Marcey stood. "I'll let you know as soon as it is over."

$$$

Shirtless and in the middle of the lawn Lil Ronnie held the smoking gun watching the spot where the van had pulled away. The blackness of the night was traded for a color of rage. Red. Red with black spots dancing before his eyes. Rage that turned his body numb. Deafened his ears and detached him from reality. The only possible thing that could snap him out of it was the voice of his kids and gradually the faint voice of his youngest started easing into his ear.

"Daddy! Daddy" multiple voices now. Lil Ronnie turned his body, getting rocked by Ty'reek and Ra'Mya. Hugging them back his eyes surveyed the street spotting Ronnie Jr, Tay and Ja'nell waking up from the sidewalk. He didn't remember them being outside until it hit him that they were returning from their walk. In a panic Lil Ronnie grabbed and ran his hand along their bodies checking all of them. Tay did a check on him as well then out of nowhere her arms squeezed him around the neck hugging him with fear. Her lips drenched with tears showered his face. For the second time that night Lil Ronnie unconsciously blocked out everything. The only thing that mattered was what was before him and sadly to say he knew one of them could have been dead. Just like Frank, just like...India's name popped into his head and Lil Ronnie broke down. His entire body collapsed to his knees but there were no tears. No weeps. He just held on to his family as tight as he could.

Ja'nell being the most clear headed one looked with an etch of worry as police sirens neared. Knowing Lil Ronnie was in shock she pulled him to his feet and started speaking. "Ronnie, the police are coming. You need to get out of here." She said with an extra tug after he showed no response in hearing her. When he did blink his way back to the present Ja'nell saw him fighting with leaving his family behind. "I got them and my license will take care of the gun now take my car and go Lil Ronnie..." She assured him. "Go!" Ja'nell pushed him, taking the gun from his hands.

Choosing right, Lil Ronnie kissed his family then dashed off toward the car.

$$$

By the time Spazz found a safe area blood had started pouring harder from Hack's torso. Hearing the white man groan Spazz turned to the steady flow of blood shaking his head. He entertained himself with the gruesome site, waiting for Tima's call back. In the meantime shit didn't make sense to him. By pictures he knew the kids belonged to Lil Ronnie along with his girl but the extra shooter had him puzzled. Looking in the rearview mirrors at the vacant lot they were parked in, he checked his phone again anxious to get out of there. Hearing another loud groan spill from Hack's mouth, Spazz couldn't help but rub his condition in his face. "Look at you. All that G.I. Joe shit, where the fuck was it, whiteboy?" A grunt or another groan or something came from Hack's lips but Spazz didn't try to understand it. "Dat shit don't work in the hood do it." He laughed but then became serious. "Who the fuck shot you?"

Hack moaned "some lad lad la...girl" he forced out. Spazz looked him over some more knowing his situation was bad. Hack's skin was already paling with a blue mixture and his breathing was getting heavier. A hospital was Hack's best option but Spazz couldn't do anything without the call from Tima first. Seeing time was of the essence he snatched his phone from the cup holder and called Tima instead. "Aye, how long before you get here dude's looking bad. We can't sit here much longer."

Tima's accent responded. He said something that made Spazz's facial expression squinch before glancing at Hack slouched in the seat. "Aight, I'm about to get the fuck out of here now. I'll see you later." He said, shifting his eyes back to the vacant lot. Double checking to make sure no one was out there he got out the van and walked over to Hack side with his gun out. When the door opened Hack's eyes bulged with awareness. He looked at the gun in Spazz's hand and started shaking his head frantically but heartlessly Spazz yanked him out of the van, dropping him to the asphalt. The barrel of his gun met Hack's face. Hack's hand rose to cover himself but before he could try his body jerked with a gunshot to the face. BOOMM! Blood splattered on the lower half of Spazz's pants. Not caring he shot him four more times then drove off to his own car.

To him the night was a waste. A complete fuck up because Lil Ronnie was suppose to be dead. 'But no pressure' he told himself "I'll finish that shit soon."

$$$

"Wuz up babygirl, why're you still up?"

Janiya felt herself move. Her head turned toward the door watching her brother stand there resembling a silhouette.

"Mommy said you took all your clothes and you're leaving us... Why?"

"Just something I have to do babygirl, changing lanes is not always a bad thing."

"Will you come back - back - back - back" an

echoing sound sounded in her head. Janiya tried shaking it away. She wanted to hear her brother. Needed to hear him but when the echoing stopped different words started rushing at her rapidly. Some of them frightening fast. "DON'T TRUST NONE OF THEM! - They killed mommy and uncle Sonny. - They're trying to KILL me. - THEY KILLED MOMMY AND UNCLE SONNY!!!" Suddenly the voice of her brother stopped. Then it was another voice. Another voice with hers. "What did he say?"

"He said you're not my friend. You killed my Mommy and uncle Sonny and now you're trying to kill him... I'm afraid."

"Janiya, don't say shit like that. There's no reason for you to be afraid."

"Did you kill him?"

"No... no-no-no-no-no-no-no-no" returned the echo and then she heard BANG! BANG!! BANG!! BANG!!! Startled, Janiya jumped clean out of her sleep. Her heart was pounding. Sweat made her bed clothes stick to her as she laid frozen holding her chest. She could never tell if the gunshots were real but that loud bang always felt terrifying. Always gave her heart that leaping thump. When she was able to admit that it was another bad dream she sat up reaching for her phone.

"It happened again." She heard herself say. Speaking in a small voice while the girls in her dorm room slept peacefully.

"I'm sorry sweetie, how bad was it this time?" Detective Greene asked.

"Bad. The voices are starting to get louder. And the gun sounds -"

"Maybe you're thinking of the trial too much. This happens when witnesses know the trial date is near. Are you having second thoughts?"

"No, he deserves to be in jail. I'm not having second thoughts."

"That's good now can you do me a big favor please?"

"Yes" Janiya replied, no longer shaken by the dream.

"We're just three days from trial and until then I want you to keep this out of your mind. Get to know the girls at the facility. Play games do whatever you have to in order to keep these dreams from happening okay."

"Will they stop once this is over?"

"Let's hope so." She heard Greene inform before letting her go.

"Three days." Janiya repeatedly gets up to use the bathroom.

$$$

Later came at 10:00 am the following morning. Spazz was in the Shores waiting for Tima. Actually he had been there since late last night and since then he had not slept or closed his mouth. For the umpteenth time Derek glanced at the bottoms of his blood splattered pants leg suggesting he go and change them.

"I am I am but that shit can wait. Were the fuck is this Arab muthafucka." He said. His voice amped as he bopped over to the window checking outside.

Everyone in the house watching looked on like he had lost half his mind. "Spazz, y'all was really trading bullets in the middle of his yard?" Asked Sabrina thrilled by it all.

"Man, toe to muthafucking toe." Turning from the window he got in his shooting stance and started imitating the night before. "When his bitch ass came out the house it was on!"

"So how the fuck you didn't hit him?" Questioned Beatup.

"Fam, you ever had big ass bullets flying your way. That shit do something to your vision." Peeking through the window agitatedly he said "the whole time this nigga shooting up his own muthafucking car trying to get at me. He didn't care bout shit."

A loud sigh came from Derek as he got tired of listening. He had been quiet as long as he could but just watching told him Spazz still didn't know what he was dealing with. "Are you listening to yourself right now! Here you are thinking shit still a game and Lil Ronnie is probably looking for you. You went at his home, Spazz!"

"I did hear people talk about their put down but that was when his friend was out." Sabrina commented.

"You talking about Mel and yeah their tight but Lil Ronnie moves on his own and this nigga just put us all in danger." Shouted Derek pointing Spazz's way.

"Aye the Arab just pulled up" Beatup acknowledged. Cutting them off as he kept watch through the window.

Tension flared between Derek and Spazz as they stared each other down. Breaking eye contact Spazz told him the famous stick to the money line then met Tima at the door.

An unpleasant grimace was spread all across Tima's face as he crossed the threshold eyeing each one of them. Seeing his gaze linger on the face unfamiliar to him Derek spoke up. "That's my man Beatup and his girl Sabrina. Their part of the hustle so it's cool."

Tima nodded but held his expression. When he looked toward Spazz he said "I gave you direct information so you can catch him at the sweetest hour. How did you fuck it up?"

Explaining as best he could Spazz started feeling foolish. Disappointment stared him down everywhere he turned and it was close to making him snap. "Who was the other shooter? Lil Ronnie doesn't keep any men with him." Tima said.

"A female but I never saw her."

"Was it Marcey?" He asked.

"Couldn't have been. We separated just before I met with Hack."

"You saw her yesterday?" Shot Tima before bellowing "I told the both of you to stay the fuck away from her! She may have fucked this up."

In denial Spazz shook his head but Derek was ready to get past it. "Listen what's done is done we just have to move on him before he catches up to us."

"And how do you suppose that? By now they know I used information from the files so Lil Ronnie will change his locations."

"Or guard them." Chimed Beatup.

"Don't matter if we catch him at the courthouse it would be unexpected." Everyone's face turned toward Derek at the mention of this so Derek continued. "Mel is his best man so he has to be at the trial. We catch him there, get the fuck out of there and we're done."

A short debate was held between themselves before agreeing it was the best they had. Spazz, still hyped, nodded at Derek for saving him then looked at Tima. "Fuck happened to you tho'?" He asked.

Grabbing the side of his face that had turned into a bruise Tima said "Signs of change. My family and I are at odds but things will continue."

"You sure?" Derek asked, not liking the confidence Tima displayed.

"Yeah. Few things must be figured out but we should be good."

"Aye that shit doesn't sound right. What are you not saying?" Derek pressed. His body stiffing with tension.

The bone underneath Tima jawline clenched. He looked at Derek ready to slang every racist slur he knew but refrained. "Just do your fucking part and you do yours." He said to Spazz adding "everything else will work out."

$$$

Work vans must have really been a style of overlooking because Pawlowski and Brad went completely unnoticed sitting across from the trap house. The van belonged to their very own department. One that looked average from the outside but held every kind of monitoring device inside. No longer did they need hand held cameras or risky drive by's. The van had lenses installed for both image and recordings. Two laptops were divided between the two and Pawlowski alternated between the screen and the van's window.

"Did you get that?" She asked. Her demeanor was as serious as it had ever been.

"If you're referring to the gun I'm checking now."

"If not I have images but recordings makes it more the realer." She said as Brad continued checking. Few seconds after hitting the rewind button he tapped her shoulder.

The footage in question shows the house door opening with Spazz standing there holding a gun. He moved to let in their guest and then closed the door behind him. "Good." We could really use that later." She informed me.

"Think the Spanish guy is their connection?"

Funny, thought Pawlowski, she had asked herself the same thing by the way he was led inside. Giving it more thought she told Brad to give her a second and started scanning images she'd taken. When the right angle of his face came up she ran it through recognition and watched as the system surfed millions of faces in a matter of seconds.

Everyone who ever was logged into their database flicked at top speed. Pawlowski waited for that funny dinging noise that would confirm the match and heard it exactly seven seconds later. "Here we go" she started to drool before her entire body froze. Her eyes looked over the image of Tima but was glued more to the bold warning sign flashing under his picture. Clicking for details it read ' SAUDI ARABIAN NATIVE WANTED FOR THE MURDERS OF... Seven faces with attaching names were under Tima Rouhani photo and there was more to read. SUSPECT IS CONNECTED TO A DEADLY DRUG FAMILY WHO HAS TIES TO SEVERAL COUNTRIES INCLUDING THE U.S. IF SPOTTED USE EXTREME CAUTION AND AVOID APPREHENDING ALONE.'

"Holly cow!" Voiced Brad once he'd read the report. "Should we call this in?"

"No that will ruin the main reasons we're here." Pawlowski replied unaffectedly. She had run across her guys of this nature and was a true believer that nailing him in the middle of his next harm was better than preventing one.

Brad looked at her. "This guy is the real deal,Pawlowski! This is who we should be after."

"He's only one of what we're after. How would you feel catching him now knowing there's more we can catch?"

"I think anyone of this magnitude should be apprehended on sight. We should call this in." He repeated.

"No Brad, we're not. Two reasons." Said Pawlowski holding up two fingers. "One of his crimes was not committed on US soil and two he'll probably be released soon as he gets back to their country. I don't want that to happen Brad, so we're going to continue sitting here until we've gotten what we came for."

Sat there they did. While he was still inside Pawlowski jotted notes confirming him as their connection. She was confident things were coming along and would not jack it off for a radio happy bust. Sometime later she saw Tima exiting with Derek and Spazz at either side of him and made sure Brad's camera was rolling. Her focus didn't leave him until he was off the street. She wouldn't dare follow him. Not when she had his tag number. Not when she knew where he had to return.

CHAPTER 19

There was a Camry sitting in Marcey driveway when she returned home. Its frame diagonally parked took up the double car space causing her to leave her out in the road. Cautiously she got out sticking a hand inside her purse where her gun was and checked the front door. Both padlocks were in place however not sure if anyone was inside she pulled the gun from her purse then opened the door after unlocking it. Lil Ronnie was seen a few steps away. He looked at her walk in then dropped his eyes back to the mess he was making in the hall.

"I'm glad you're here, are you okay?" She said, Closing the door behind her while easing the gun back into her purse.

"So you heard?" He asked her.

Seeing his hard unreadable eyes boring she looked away but hugged his body. "Yes i did and things sounded a mess I was so afraid." She said,

"Funny I didn't see any missed calls from you." She heard him reply before feeling his hands shove her away. The force made her step back and prior to looking at his face she thought he was angry with her. Her eyes raced the answer but there was only pain in his eyes.

Diverting her gaze to the floor she asked "Why are you pulling your stuff from the closet?"

"Looking for the gun and it's not in there. I've looked everywhere." Lil Ronnie said this frustratedly.

"That gun was left under the mattress so I got rid of it but here." She said giving him the gun she put back in her purse.

Taking the gun from her hand he examined it then leaned against the wall sliding down to the floor. His head fell inside his hands and Marcey heard a sob. "I was shooting right in their direction, Marcey. My entire family caught in the middle because one of you gave up my address." The gun was held against his head as he kept his hands in place however, its closeness did not put fear into her.

Scooting to his level she picked his head up for him to look at her. "I'm not going to lie to you. The information came from our side and I did everything I could to stop it."

"Why?" asked Lil Ronnie, his voice squeezing between pain and a cry.

"On the phone when we last spoke, this is what I wanted to talk to you about. Tima found out about Derek and Spazz now their under his wing and killing you was his first priority."

"You could have told me. What if Eclipse would have been there then what?!"

"Nothing would have changed. I didn't tell you because we had just gotten over our shit and I didn't need this for us. But the minute I put things together I've been on them. I knew their every move, Ronnie."

He went silent. She could tell he was angry with her. Could almost see thoughts racing through his mind. But more than anything his mind couldn't get past the danger brought to his family. "All this shit I've done for your family. You, Hazik all you muthafuckas and y'all sit back knowing this shit was about to happen."

Placing her hands along his, Marcey removed the gun then spoke with absolute sincerity. "This is all Tima. No one else was in on this and for his actions Hazik made it clear whatever happens to him happens. There are no consequences for retribution."

Lil Ronnie's head came up. His dark pupils stared at her as what she just said registered. "Where is he?" He wanted to know.

"Right now I'm not sure. He left sometime last night but finding him won't be hard."

There was another pause. Lil Ronnie's mind started working then he looked at her. " Marcey, you were there weren't you? At my house."

"The first two shots was mine. A warning to both you and Tay. She covered the kids soon as she heard the shot." Seeing him rewinding the scene in his head Marcey answered before he could ask. "I shot the white guy but I don't know if he's dead."

"Where was Derek?"

"Derek is not moving like Spazz or Tima. He's interested in money, not bloodshed."

Grabbing the gun from her before coming to his feet Marcey saw him tuck it under his shirt. "I'm killing anyone involved. Derek, Tima, Spazz and anyone else who didn't stop harm from coming near my family."

"Tima will be a problem for you. Let me deal with him my way." She asked?

Close to saying no she saw him turn his back "you got until I kill the rest of these muthafuckas."

Taking it, Marcey pushed, Derek is valuable. Killing him will only leave more work for you to do in the streets. Think of reconsidering." She said.

"What the fuck is you talking about. I did all my considering and if he didn't want bloodshed he should have never came to you."

"And I'm not arguing with you but for one second think of business after this madness is over. Who will be your feet when it's time for you to kick back. Big Blue arms extend across the city. Derek arms are spreading. Adding him gives you multiple cities. He'll turn Ronnie. Derek will do whatever you tell him if you're willing to accept him."

"I don't trust him Marcey, never have."

"Then trust me. Let me make this decision." she begged.

A thought crossed Lil Ronnie's mind as he walked to the back room collecting his keys. He didn't share his thoughts with her until the front door opened and he was half out the door. "Take care of your uncle. That's all I care about right now."

"And you do the same with Spazz. I'm here if you need me, Ronnie."

Watching him get into the car driving away Marcey closed the door and took a seat behind it. Battle after battle after battle he was being put through and each one made her love him more. Securing him was securing her future and that was Marcey's thoughts as she started to devise a remedy for her uncle.

$$$

Wanting her task over and done with, Marcey got back inside her car driving to Delray. Her uncle along with Derek were the only people on her mind and neither of them she would play with. Derek having the luxury of two options would either agree to her terms or meet an untimely demise. Tima however is not so lucky. Since the order had been given to handle him she had no other option but to do so. It was a price he knew he'd pay and she planned to do him just as she did Bell.

Her thoughts were shortened by scarce traffic as she pulled into the trap house drive cutting off her engine. Parked in front of her were Derek's Tahoe and the Trailblazer, knowing who the vehicles belonged to, Marcey got out and walked to the door. Sabrina opened it after the first knock and one look at her expression told Marcey they must have been discussing her. Ignoring the look she stepped in finding Derek on the couch.

"He's not here, Marcey." She heard Derek say soon as the door closed.

"That's fine." she said, clearing her throat. "I'm here for you."

"Look I told you-"

"Derek." Marcey called, cutting him off. Her voice rose a little and she felt Sabrina become erect beside her. Shooting her a warning glare Marcey looked back at Derek "You asked me for a chance and I gave it." Marcey said. Standing where she was. "Your numbers did good and your humbleness has not been overlooked. I'm here for that reason, only now you can accept another chance of mine and come speak with me or I will walk out dusting my hands." She said, Marcey didn't look to her right where Beatup stood nor did she look back at Sabrina. Marcey kept her eyes on Derek hoping he made the right decision. When no signs of disapproval came she turned around and led the way outside.

"Make this shit quick Marcey, I got shit to do and your face ain't welcome round here." He said once they were outside by the cars.

"Fair enough." Marcey replied but took time before speaking another word. She looked at all the vehicles lined along the street gathering her thoughts. What she needed to accomplish with Derek was important. Coupling him with Lil Ronnie meant everything she had explain to Lil Ronnie. No more risk and exposure. Just money. Money and family. "You told me you didn't want shit to do with any blood spilling so why didn't you warn me they were headed to kill Lil Ronnie?"

"It ain't my fucking business, Marcey! In case you forgot me and Lil Ronnie is on two different sides of the field."

"It doesn't have to be that way."

"You're right but that's the way he made it. Look if that's all you came for you need to bounce."

A rush of anger ripped through Marcey but she tried hiding it to keep peace. Glancing at the parked vehicles again for distraction she examined them while reminding herself of patients.

"No disrespect but you blowing hot air ain't what I came out here for, so is you done?"

Her eyes stayed on the street. Every car looked as if it had been in countless rounds with some kind of auto mechanic. The only vehicle seemed to be up to par was the strange looking work van sitting directly across from them. Marcey looked at it for some time then focused on Derek. "You're right so let me cut to the chase. This thing with my uncle is going nowhere fast. He's not business oriented and you know this." Marcey let her words form an effect then said "I can give you a more secure position. Almost like before only this time Lil Ronnie will know."

"And then what work for him?"

"No. You'll work with him" Stamped Marcey. "You and Lil Ronnie won't even have to speak. No one is over you and you can expand far as you want with as much dope as you need."

Derek thought about it but shook his head. "I can't turn my back on Spazz, he's my nigga Marcey, and that comes before money."

"You think Lil Ronnie is going to let him live after last night? Spazz and whoever is with him is the walking dead."

The truth held thick in the air and both her and Derek gazes went to the street. Marcey's in particular went directly back to the work van. "Death can fall both ways." Derek said leaving her by the cars.

"You're a smart individual Derek, allow the opportunity to linger before you make the wrong decision." The house door closed and Marcey backed out of the drive neither happy or sad. The coming events would force his hand Derek just didn't know it yet. Putting her gear in drive Marcey pulled away but not before giving the van one more look. When she turned off the street her mind was still on the van. It was the antenna for her and rather than leave the neighborhood she made a u-turn and circled the block.

$$$

"You think she saw us?" Brad asked, watching the rear bumper of Marcey car turn off the street.
Snatching her headphones off Pawlowski slung them on the table boiling. "Of course she fucking saw us. She particularly looked me right in the eyes!"
"Then why aren't we moving?" Brad asked.
"Because it's a dead giveaway and I'm not completely sure she saw us."
A couple seconds later Pawlowski nearly pulled a muscle in her back when a knocking sound came on the side of the van. "Fuck" Jumped Brad nearly

pulling the laptop off the table with him. They looked at each other as the knocking continued, then Pawlowski signaled for him to check. "Its her." He confirmed with a blown expression.

From her seat Pawlowski stayed put soaking in complete disbelief. Who the hell would come to a van knowing the police were inside of it. MARCEY her mind shouted with anger. Pawlowski sat there as long as she could, listening to the perpetual knocking turn into a bang that pivoted her to her feet. "Are you about to let her in?" Brad asked and Pawlowski stopped to glare at him.

"I don't think we have a choice. Close the laptop off and don't let her see what we're doing." Turning back for the door Pawlowski slid it open in the middle of Marcey banging.

"Pawlowski!" Marcey said before smiling. "I knew this van belonged to law enforcement but I didn't expect you inside of it. Slate has let you loose again huh?"

"Hate to burst your bubble but we're not here for you Marcey. This assignment is unrelated to anything you have going, now can you please go away before our cover is blown?" Pawlowski asked as nicely as she could.

Marcey looked at her then inside the van. "Somehow I doubt that."

"It's the truth" Pawlowski said, blocking Marcey's vision. "Are you going to leave willingly or do I need to pull out cuffs?"

"You can't arrest a concerned civilian."

"Cut the shit, Marcey." Pawlowski said, rolling her eyes. "What do you want?"

"There's a problem I'm having and solving it may be exactly what someone like you needs."

"Don't be ridiculous. What I need is for people like you to stay out of my life." Shot Pawlowski.

" Okay" Marcey said, not backing away from the van. "Then I'll take my time and speak here but that won't be a good look if that house you're watching see's me here. It can blow whatever you're investigation." Giving her a second to think Marcey urged "let me in, Pawlowski."

The van was a tight fit. Sitting in her seat was the only way Marcey could enter. Telling her to close the door Pawlowski felt her skin itch from their closeness. "You're in now say what you have to say and be done with it, Marcey."

"Hey I remember you." Marcey said ignoring Pawlowski to look at Brad. "You was my tail right?"

"Sorry about that. I was-"

"Brad!" Shouted Pawlowski. Cutting her eyes between them.

Marcey Rouhani, get on with it and you." Said Pawlowski eyeing Brad "don't you say a another word to her."

Sighing with a whiner's remorse Marcey said. "Don't be rude, Pawlowski. You and I don't have to always be at separate ends, as a matter a fact I'm here taking the first step."

"Our positions were sealed before Selvester's death during your home wrecking."

"Then let's at least agree he's much better where he is.'

This got Pawlowski out of her seat. His slender frame and enormous breast stood body to body with Marcey taking the van for all its space. "Don't you ever fucking disrespect him in death. You didn't deserve him and you-"

"Ladies!" Called Brad prying his arm between them for separation. When a hairs gap was visible he said "you, you're in the van hopefully to help now give else what you have so we can all move on."

Both women looked at Brad take charge and then Marcey devolved "There is someone I may know with outstanding warrants from another country. Making the arrest can do some good."

"We know about your uncle, Marcey. Watched him leave a little before your arrival. We're not interested." Pawlowski informed.

"Arresting him will save lives probably his own."

"What, is he in your way Marcey? Went against the family code or something? I know how these things go. Your kind don't give information for nothing."

"Call it a motherly consciousness taking place."

"Take it to someone else."

A stare down came. Two spoiled women piss

fighting because neither would budge. Then Marcey broke eye contact. "Fine!" She said, "This is your job you're throwing away. The moment I go to Slate and inform him that your personal vendetta against me caused you to neglect your duties you'll both be history. Will you let her make that decision for you?" Marcey asked Brad.

The young stud's eyes were shaking faster than he could his head. He looked like he was about to burst. Unafraid but aware of the truth Pawlowski relented with a flush of hot air escaping her lungs. "Run a tag location and gain his whereabouts." She barked.

Ten minutes later Pawlowski was back alone inside the van with Brad. Marcey had left satisfied and the effect left her feeling raped. It took Brad to call her name several times before she snapped out of it.

"I think this is a good idea besides Detective Greene told you to get what you can." Nodding Pawlowski shook her funk and climbed in the driver's seat. "Where are we going?" He asked.

"It's over. We'll take the credit for the capture. Write the reports and see what's next."

Not the victory she wanted. Pawlowski floored the van and for the very first time accepted it was time to move on.

CHAPTER 20

The courtroom was the same exact room Finnerty held Mel's jury selection, evidentiary hearing and all other prior hearings. Before them would be the same heartless judge and blood thirsty prosecutors. The jury was present and to the left. Sitting in the jury pool looking acute and amp for action. Across from them were the bailiffs, word typist and court's assistants. Splitting them were the judge's chambers which is where she was at this very moment. Finnerty and the state's prosecutor represented the other half of the courtroom and behind them were the audience. Family of victims, news reporters and so forth. The place was crowded at standing room only and as Finnerty swept their faces he felt himself become alive and ready.

"Have my client arrived yet?" He asked. Walking over to the bailiffs in a thousand dollar suit.

"In the back." The baliff said before informing, "You have about fifteen minutes before the judge comes out."

Taking it, Finnerty walked through a door where detainees were held and found Mel pacing in one of the tiny cells.

"Sleep well last night?" He asked, referring to the conversation they held the day before.

"Nawl she's still on my mind." Mel admitted.

Biting his bottom lip Finnerty grabbed one of the bars and shoved his other hand in his pocket. "Sorry to hear that. But look at it on the bright side, all of this is almost over."

"Yeah I know, I just don't want her going through it. That stand will make her replay all that shit, not just today, but throughout life. I rather she just moved on nah'mean."

"There isn't much we could do there. The state is gonna call her and will certainly squeeze her for all they can. Then I have to get up there and do the same. It's going to get ugly but that's how it goes."

"Nawl man, I ain't feeling that." Said Mel who despite his mental disarray looked crisp on his day of judgment. "There has to be something we could do."

Clueless Finnerty shook his head and tried

wrapping things up. "Aight well all of your family is in place. Including your mother, is there anything you want me to tell them before we start trial?"

Mel ignored the question. He sat down feeling weighed by Janiya's testimony. Finnerty watched for a second or two but after checking his watch decided to step. "Finnerty." Mel called holding him. "Ask the prosecutor if we agree to not cross examine Janiya on the stand would they just allow her tell her story. That way she can get all of this out her system once and for all."

"Sure I can ask." Finnerty replied. "But cross and recross is part of the process and may I remind you not pressing the witness could really hurt the case."

"I'm guilty man." Stated Mel. His tired and stressed eyes found Finnerty. "Just figure that shit out and leave the aftermath to me."

Nodding Finnerty walked away after Mel turned his back feeling his readiness evaporate. He should have stayed his ass in the courtroom he thought before shoving the door open flopping down at the defense table.

$$$

The courthouse parking areas were divided into six sections. You had both top and bottom parking garages then Dixie and Federal Hwy. Then

Austrasia blvd all the way to Tamarind avenue. There were more than five hundred cars to account for so when Derek reached the courthouse his focus was more on the inside rather than the out. Planning ahead he had Sabrina already inside waiting for Lil Ronnie's arrival to follow him out. Using the meter onside of the road they parked right on the main street then shut off the engine.

The opportunity Marcey laid on him had definitely resurfaced in his mind. If he didn't have his partnership with Spazz along with Tima's word swallowing his pride would not have been a problem. But he was true to his team and that's the only thing that had him out there strapped and ready to end Lil Ronnie's life. When an alert came to Spazz's phone Derek looked his way. "Is that Tima?" He asked. Repeating the same question he'd asked several times that morning.

"Nawl not yet, maybe the injury is getting to him. His old ass should have been up." Spazz said after checking his phone.

"Beatup, see if Lil Ronnie is in there. He should have showed up by now." Derek went on to say and to be honest the questions were more out of nervousness than anything. Every time he looked out of his window a police car was present. It was your typical courthouse activity but you couldn't tell that to someone driving a car loaded with guns. "Beatup, what she say?"

"Fam, Sabrina gone hit back as soon as she sees him. Chill the fuck out!" Spazz answered instead.

"This shit is straight clown work. Why the fuck you didn't just let the beef go from jump we wouldn't be in this mess." The statement made both Beatup and Spazz glare at him. He knew he was bugging, and holding all the shit with Marcey to himself seemed to make it worse. Derek just wanted the shit over with. He wasn't confused by bipolar or none of that. "Is that him?!" His voice jumped looking at Spazz's phone alerting him again.

"Nawl and don't ask me no more."

"Then who is it?" He asked, frowning.

Snatching his phone Spazz looked at it then dropped it back in his lap. "It's wifey. I'll get back to her later."

"Nawl man, handle that so she'll stop calling." He waited for Spazz to call back then looked back out the window. He didn't want to do this shit. He already had the death of his babymomma on his hands and that fucked with him every night. He knew what murder brought but when you were swimming with certain sharks it became the only resolution. Fuck! He thought before Spazz interrupted his thought process.

"Aye Fam, something just popped up at the house I need you to swing me by the crib." Although his every action that morning spelled indecision

Derek looked at Spazz like he was now the one bugging, however that all changed when he looked into his friend's eyes. Without another word being said Derek remained quiet and put his truck back on the road.

$$$

Lisa hand held Ms.Betty's firmly as they took their seats. They both looked around at all the unfamiliar faces present and Lisa could have sworn she saw Ms.Betty smiling.

"You're okay?" Lisa asked, squeezing her hand.

"Oh yes, today ain't sad at all. I was just thinking all this time Mel thought he was fooling me." She laughed. "The minute y'alls Ma Anne left this earth and you two had to fein for each other I knew the world was for a wreck and my Mel wouldn't be far behind it. But look at all this people present like they were in his football days." Lisa looked with her at the unfamiliar faces again but knew this was Ms.Betty way of seeing the good. "I was mad and hurt but now I ain't. My baby is a somebody." Agreeing, Lisa continued to hold her silence until hearing the bailiff escorting Mel out.

The first glimpse of her son made Ms.Betty jump to her feet shouting his name. Lisa joined and then Tay and Ja'nell and all of their sisters. Strangers looked and pointed cameras but neither of them quieted until Mel turned round smiling and the bailiff was lashing threats. After the courtroom was settled and Mel ushered in his seat the room was given one last order to rise before the judge.

"You all may be seated" they all heard Judge Brown pronounce before she took her seat.

"Your Honor, we hereby present the case of Melvin Johnson" Said the prosecutor standing momentarily to state her case. "Case #4567882QG3."

"Very well you may be seated." Judge Brown replied before saying "Counsel?"

"Jack Finnerty Your Honor, on behalf of my client Mr. Melvin Johnson case #4567288QG3."

"And are both parties ready?" Lisa heard her ask and couldn't help but look over her shoulder at the door. Seeing Lil Ronnie had not arrived she took a deep breath and held Ms.Betty hand tighter."

"Yes Your Honor, we are."

$$$

"Please!!! I did what you asked, Pleaaaase!" Maria cried, straining against the duck tape that had her arms and legs bound. "Just let me and my kids go and I won't say anything. Please!" She looked at the three masked men after the phone had been snatched from her ear prepared to do anything. From one to the other her begging continued until Red had gotten enough and taped her mouth. Then as if that wasn't enough he dragged her out of the room and shoved her back inside the closet where they were keeping her. When the door was secure Hot lifted his mask and walked in the next room. "Let the boss know he should see him in half an hour."

$$$

"Ladies and gentlemen, the day of February 6, 2016 is a day many would never forget. It was a night violent gunshots interrupted the perfect evening for those out trying to dine in this wonderful city. A night that turned unsafe for those same individuals. A night one lost his life leaving many to cry all because of one man's actions." The prosecutor's voice softened as her finger pointed at Mel but everyone inside the room felt the disdain. She continued "What you are about to see and hear right in this courtroom will make you carry the same hatred as myself for criminals like him. It will cause you to hate guns as well as the people who use them." Her words ended abruptly this time. Her sandals walked small steps letting the crowd feel her before opening her mouth again. "I want to thank you all for being present at a time when society needs you most. Hopefully you people of the jury will see the logic in holding someone of this nature accountable." strutting back over to her seat she let the jury see her stare at Mel before shaking her head pitifully.

Finnerty rose from his seat. He did so while giving the prosecutor a zealous hand clap for her Oscar winning speech but made it a point as he turned to the jury without a smile. "I beg to differ.... See we as people are raised in different ethnic backgrounds. Some of us, like the prosecutor here, have never cursed. Never ran a red light or even sneezed for that matter. Let her tell it being less than perfect is illogical and logical is being perfect. My, so many of us are perfect." He teased, causing the jury to stir in light humor. "You hear that peers." Finnerty said, cuffing his ear with his hand drawing attention to the jury's snickers. "Sounds like they agree that none of us are perfect. Not me. Not you. And neither is he!" Finnerty informed Mel out. "Please if the residents of this fine State have heard nothing so far, hear me and hate no one. Thank you." The short walk back to the table was done in silence. When he sat he looked at all the people of the jury eyeing him. To say any good would come of it was premature but for now he nodded and prepared for the next phase.

For almost two hours they listened to the redundant materials prosecution used to bolster their evidence. Numerous officers who arrived far after the scene testified. Then forensics and store managers as well as employees. It was a hundred and twenty minutes of boredom before Judge Brown told the prosecution to prepare their last and final witness. Knowing exactly who that witness would be, the courtroom roared in murmurs. This is what most of the people came for. Everyone wanted to see Janiya's testimony so much so that the noise continued rising until the judge banged her gravel calling recess.

"The testimony will take place after recess and I expect everyone to be on their best behavior."

$$\$\$\$$$

The Tahoe drove with the same intensity spilling from Spazz aura. Derek switched from lane to lane while watching his mirrors. Today had went from confusing to fucked up and Derek needed to know what was going on. "Bruh, I'm not trying to get in your business but what the fuck is the emergency?" He asked. Flooring it down the highway.

"My youngest man, the lil nigga swallowed some shit I left behind and now Maria says he's foaming an'shit. Threatening to call the law."

"Fuck!" Derek said. "Why would you leave some shit anyway you know how kids is."

"I know I know, but forget that and listen. You and Beatup have to get back to the courthouse. If that nigga get away today there's no telling when we'll catch him feel'me?"

Frustration flooded Derek's face but he knew there wasn't any other way. Nodding his head reluctantly he exited off the highway turning on Spazz street. "Look Fam, I'm serious no fuck ups. Soon as I can get free I'm on my way aight?" He said once Derek stopped in front of his house.

Giving Derek a dap-hug Spazz did the same with Beatup after they were out the car then started walking toward his house. Just like the previous times his head and eyes were only in the direction he was going. Making it to his doorstep Spazz unlocked the door then walked in calling their names. Receiving silence he began to think they had taken off for the hospital and started looking for any sign Maria may have left behind.

$$\$\$\$$$

"Court proceedings have resumed. Prosecution, you may call your final witness."

The prosecutor stood to do so however after getting a final warning from Mel Finnerty stood first to address the courts. "Your Honor, please pardon me for a moment. My client is in a position to lose his freedom for the remainder of his life and despite my advice his concerns are for the sanity of this young girl that's about to testify. Questioning will brutalize her and-"

"Counsel, is there a suggestion here?"

"Yes Your Honor, but the request is odd probably has never been done inside of a courtroom but if yourself and prosecution agree we would consider the young girl telling her story without either side interrupting."

The courtroom seemed mystified for a minute then the judge snapped out of it and looked at the prosecutor. "Very well then. Bring out your witness."

Detective Greene came walking down the aisle holding Janiya's hand until the prosecution took over and led her to the stand. The crowd saw her look over all of them one by one before spotting and locking her eyes on Mel. The two held each other's gaze for a few seconds before the prosecutor interfered. "Hello Janiya, do you mind telling the people inside this courtroom how you met Melvin?"

Janiya nodded "my mom and I was at the shopping plaza and when we got ready to leave the car wouldn't start so he helped us."

"What happened after that?"

"My mother and Mel started dating and he started coming around everyday. I think him and my mother was having sex and my brother didn't like it." Janiya checked around the courtroom to see if she should continue and after getting the nod she went on. "It caused my mother and brother to have a big fight and my brother left. When he came back it was real late outside and he was being real quiet to not wake mommy." A lump formed in Janiya's throat as she thought of her next words. Tears were seen soaking her eyes instantly but bravely she looked at Mel as they both knew what she was about to say. "We talked for a while and then he had to go but when he made it downstairs loud gunshots started. "I couldn't see anyone but I heard voices...and then I heard nothing." Janiya's hands shot to her face as she said it but her tears overflowed them. Detective Greene came to help her out and eventually Janiya got back under control.

"What happened after that, Janiya?"

"I didn't want to be alone and the silence was scaring me. So I walked downstairs and saw my uncle Sonny bleeding on the couch. When I went to check on him I saw my mother laying in her doorway. She was.... They killed my mommy!" Janiya yelled. She shut her eyes and cried louder than before. The judge looked to the prosecutor and the prosecutor looked to Greene to see if they needed to take Janiya off the stand but Greene knew what Janiya wanted. Calming her once again Greene took over the questioning. "Who did this, Janiya?"

"Him!" She said sternly. Looking and pointing at Mel.

"How do you know, Janiya?"

"Because they killed my brother too and my brother told me they did."

"And when your brother told you this what did you do?"

"I told Mel and he promised it wasn't true. He said he would never harm anyone."

"And then what happened?"

Before answering, Janiya looked at Mel. Hatred built in her eyes. Betrayal was in her eyes. Every evil spirit a fifteen year old could muster lived in her for Mel. She watched him sit there for as long as she could before hearing Greene repeat the question. "We went out to eat but when we got there he had to go back outside."

"Why?"

"To kill someone else."

"Did you see him, Janiya? Did you see that man right there kill this time?" The question came from the prosecutor and Janiya looked at her relieved to know her answer meant something.

"Yes" she said, bringing the courtroom to an uproar.

$$$

"For those of you who have been listening, I will not hinder you with my words. We see the hurt in that young girl's eyes. We heard her cry. Someone as little as her gets to inherit all the troubles of a parentless child. All because of one man. Ladies and gentlemen the person behind this may not be perfect like myself as his lawyer stated earlier but he does know right from wrong and wrong is what we're up against!" The prosecutor took a long lasting look at the jury then went to her seat.

Judge Brown moved to the next phase of closing arguments and that was to call the defense for their closing arguments however a delay occurred when Mel pulled Finnerty by the arm and whispered something in his ear. Finnerty looked at him with more disagreement but followed orders and stood to speak. "Your Honor, the defense has nothing further. We can go into deliberation."

$$$

Hot waited. Red waited. Even Tank was on chill as Spazz continued making his way into the house. They could see he was strapped and to keep everything in their control they all found someplace to hide. Hot was the only one able to keep him in sight which was perfect from how the house was designed. In total there were four bedrooms with an extra door for the closet and restroom. Across from the restroom is where Maria was left and the room beside her held the kids and inside that room the television was left on to keep them calm. The television drew Spazz attention. Hot saw him look toward the noise then motioned for Red to get ready. Red signaled Tank and collectively they followed the count of Hot fingers. Each step Spazz took Hot would lift a finger. Spazz hand reached the knob just as Hot made it to the third finger and from nowhere a fast charging Hot clocked him with the butt of his gun. Spazz's lengthy size dropped to one knee but before a groan could escape from his mouth Tank rushed pinning his arms into a figure-four.

"What the fuck!" Spazz hollered through the arm lock. He tried to move but Tank had the weight and power advantage. The gun went across his face again. Hot watch thick clots of blood gush from his wound before relieving Spazz of his gun. Seeing all was under control Red went and tapped on the kids door and out walked Lil Ronnie holding the youngest in his arms.

Lil Ronnie told Tank to hold up Spazz head and the instant Spazz saw Lil Ronnie with his child he began to buck. The efforts were futile but it did cause the child to cry however Lil Ronnie ignored it. "You think shooting over my kids heads is safe, nigga?" Lil Ronnie asked before telling Red to pass him a set of clippers.

Knowing what was coming Hot and Tank fought until they were able to move Spazz to the couch and duck tape him and only then did Lil Ronnie open the closet door and hand the child to his mother.

"Answer me!" Shouted Lil Ronnie soon as he was back in the living room with the cutters.

"Fuck you, you-" WHAM!! Came Lil Ronnie's fist hitting Spazz right in the mouth. Blood poured from both areas of his face however he didn't groan this time. He was a nigga for pain thought Lil Ronnie but that was okay. Lil Ronnie was there because it was what the streets wanted. See the streets do not lose respect. They remember the respected but only on the level you place yourself. Back when Lil Ronnie was a kid knowledge belonged to his mentor. His very first shot at street recognition Frank made him go out and buy every fashionable thing the streets wanted. That was an act that told the streets Lil Ronnie was boss material. And this was the same thing just at a different angle. The fashion on this level was murder. A gruesome show. One the streets would respect for the rest of their lives and Lil Ronnie knew just how to separate himself from the amateurs as well as the elite. He was about to place his status in it's very own category, period.

With the clippers in his hands he walked over to Spazz and began cutting into his fingers slowly. Spazz screams shot throughout the house causing his family to cry out as well but again Lil Ronnie ignored it. When the blade had severed each finger the toes came next. Spazz cried, Spazz pleaded, Spazz passed out realizing this person who he thought was a kid wasn't one. He was everything Derek warned but it was too late. Cold water awoke him after he had fainted and seeing Lil Ronnie working on his other foot made him start begging. "Please man, you got- got it-Arrrghhh!" Came another cry after Lil Ronnie clipped his sixth toe. The other four came soon after and he heard Lil Ronnie ordering him to be untaped.

"Get up!" Yelled Lil Ronnie.

"I can't!" Spazz told him after a failed attempt.

Not having it Lil Ronnie had the front door opened then threatened to kill Spazz children if he didn't try harder. Spazz tried again but without any toes his balance was off making him fall immediately. Hot helped by dragging him out to the middle of the street for everyone to see. "This is what the fuck you wanted!" Lil Ronnie yelled, wanting everyone out there to hear and know what was going on. Aiming his gun at Spazz head Lil Ronnie said his final words "tell them muthafuckers where you going to warn their people bout fucking with me." BOOM... BOOM BOOM BOOM Every bullet the gun held went into Spazz's body. His head, face, neck and chest all gained enough steel to leave him bloated. When there wasn't anything else on Spazz to kill Lil Ronnie ordered his family dead then pulled off.

$$$

In the southern district of Florida this courtroom found Melvin Johnson Jr guilty in the first degree. As sworn under oath I judge Lucy Brown sentence you to the maximum penalty of this crime. The court by right sentenced Melvin Johnson Jr to life imprisonment with the possibility of parole. Take care yourself Mr Johnson and I wish you the best of luck."

EPILOGUE

People were piling out of the courtroom in a stampede. Sad faces, blink faces and faces that were well known to Derek but no Lil Ronnie. Waiting across the street in the Tahoe Derek watched Lisa and Tay walking away with Mel's mother but again no Lil Ronnie. Something was not right. This was a day his man met judgment, a day your best friend would not miss. A day similar to your funeral, where you had to pay your respects. Believing he had overlooked Lil Ronnie, Derek told Beatup he was getting out and opened his door to do so. As soon as his feet touched the ground and his door closed an all black SUV swerved so close the tires nearly nipped his toes. Derek mugged the tinted windows but saw nothing except his own reflection. A creepy second passed before the passenger window descended revealing Marcey's beautiful face. She stared at him. Her face highlighted with dark eyeliner surrounded by her black rich hair. For some reason there was an unfamiliar beat in Derek's chest. Maybe because he was here to kill her man and she had to somehow know. He himself did not know, but as their eyes remained locked he notice her lips moving. "That ticking time bomb has exploded. You now work for us, any questions?" She asked in more of a statement. Derek mind was still occupied with wondering how she knew where he was but outwardly he felt his head nodding.

"Good. There were fifty delivered to your home address. From there you distribute as you please but pay on time with the precise amount. Any questions?" Marcey asked again. Her solid demeanor almost made it hard for him to think. No longer was she the Marcey he saw around Spazz. Spazz had almost made her obtain a desperate appeal. The woman he stood in front of now exuded power. That mafia power.

"What about Lil Ronnie?" He ask, swallowing a lump that had formed in his throat.

Soon as he spoke the back glass came down and Lil Ronnie's forearm rested outside the window. His stare carried the same seriousness as Marcey's only deeper. "Anymore questions?" Derek heard Marcey ask pulling his gaze back to her!

The Story Of Marcey coming SOON!!

Made in United States
Orlando, FL
22 November 2023

39227192R20166